True Ghost Stories & Hauntings: Real Catholic Exorcisms

by
Scott L. Smith

True Ghost Stories & Hauntings: Real Catholic Exorcisms
by Scott L. Smith
Copyright © 2020 Holy Water Books

ISBN-13: 978-1-950782-18-5
All rights reserved.
Holy Water Books (Publisher)

No part of this book may be reproduced, or stored in a retrieval system, or transmitted in any form or by any means, electronic, mechanical, photocopying, recording, or otherwise, without the express written permission of the author(s) and/or editor(s).

None is vanquished in this spiritual combat,
but he who ceases to struggle and loses confidence in God.
"He does not receive the Victor's Crown unless he fights well"
(2 Timothy 2:5)

Please pray before reading...

Prayer of St. Michael the Archangel

Saint Michael Archangel,
defend us in battle,
be our protection against the wickedness
and snares of the devil;
may God rebuke him, we humbly pray;
and do thou, O Prince of the heavenly host,
by the power of God, cast into hell
Satan and all the evil spirits
who prowl through the world
seeking the ruin of souls.
Amen.

Table of Contents

Introduction 1
Emma Schmidt, 1926-28 5

    Earling, Iowa: A Quiet Railroad Town 7
    Witchcraft & Curses Open the Door 9
    The Exorcist, Father Theophilus Riesinger 12
    The Exorcisms Begin 16
    The Dramatic End 19

Roland Doe, 1949 21

    The Impact of *The Exorcist* 23
    Not Mount Rainier 24
    Don't Play With Ouija Boards 26
    The Need for a Priest 29
    The First Exorcist: Father Edward Hughes 32
    The Exorcisms 33
    The Second Round of Exorcisms: An Old Priest & a Young Priest 35
    He Is Gone 39

Anneliese Michel, 1976 41

    A Devout Young Catholic 41
    The Torments Begin 44
    The Shrine at San Damiano 46
    The Exorcists 49
    The Last Days Before Exorcism 53
    The Exorcisms Begin 56
    Demons Terrorized by the Rosary 58
    Transcripts of Lucifer and Judas 60
    Testing Anneliese 61
    The End & Our Lady of Fatima 62
    A Matter for the Law 64
    An Unofficial Saint 65

Nicola Aubrey, 1565 67

Introduction: The Apologetical Exorcism 67
Father Muller's Account of the Vervins Exorcism 69
The Exorcist: Father de Motta 70
Failed Exorcisms by Calvinists 70
The Second Round of Exorcisms 74
The Real Presence of 78
Jesus in the Eucharist 78
Satan is Expelled 80

Appendix I: *The Roman Ritual of Exorcism*, Chapter One, "Instructions for Exorcising Those Possessed by Evil Spirit" 82
Appendix II: "Begone Satan!" by Father Carl Vogl 88

   Foreward 90
   Begone Satan! 92
   Recent Case of Possession and Expulsion in Earling, Iowa 94
   The Lady in Question 97
   The Decisive Moment Had Arrived 101
   One or More Devils 105
   The Demon Jacob 110
   Acute Cause of the Devil's Pain 113
   Holy Water 113
   Little Flower of the Child Jesus 114
   St. Michael 115
   Crucifix and Relic of the Cross 115
   Antipathy Against The Whole Procedure 117
   The Experience of His Life 119
   Satan's Speeches 122
   Satan's Knowledge Can Be Embarrassing 122
   Dumb Devils and Avenging Spirits 126
   Avenging Spirits 126
   Night Prowlers 127
   How the Possessed Woman Fared 129
   Exorcism Lasted Twenty-Three Days 130
   High Commander 130
   Antichrist 131

More Atonement 134
  Battles Between Good and Evil Spirits 135
  The Little Flower of the Child Jesus 135
  The Devils Depart 136
  Theresa Neumann 138
  Letter from Dr. John Dundon 140
Appendix III: About the Author 142
  More from Scott Smith 143
  What You Need to Know About Mary But Were Never Taught 146
  Catholic Nerds Podcast 147
  The Catholic ManBook 148
  The Seventh Word 149
  Blessed is He Who … Models of Catholic Manhood . 150

Introduction

EXORCIZO, te, immundissime spiritus, omnis incursio adversarii, omne phantasma, omnis legio. (I cast thee out, thou unclean spirit, along with the least encroachment of the wicked enemy, and every phantom and diabolical legion.)

—*from* the Rite of Exorcism, the Roman Ritual of the Catholic Church

The words above are given power, not by the ancient language they are written in, nor from their author or any magical incantation, but from Jesus, Himself, the one who founded the Church, which empowers its priests to expel demons and even Satan, himself, with these words.

There was a time in the middle of the last century when it became considered foolish to believe Satan existed, and so exorcism fell out of fashion. But fashions leave little imprint on the Church, nor is the Church duped by prevailing sentiments.

Nevertheless, the Church has proceeded with exorcisms prudently, embracing the truths of medical science and investigating alleged cases of possession for other, merely natural causes. Certain signs and symptoms help distinguish between natural and supernatural origins of illness.

The Roman Ritual of Exorcism cites several specific signs of possession:

Above all, [the exorcist] must not easily believe that someone is possessed by an Evil Spirit. [The exorcist] must be thoroughly acquainted with those signs by which he can distinguish the possessed person from those who suffer from a physical illness. The signs of possession by Evil Spirit are of a peculiar genre. Among others; when the subject speaks unknown languages with many words or understands unknown languages; when he clearly knows about things that are distant or hidden; when he shows a physical strength far above his age or normal condition. These manifestations together with others of the same kind are major indications.[1]

Others symptoms include revulsion to holy objects or to subjects of a religious nature, foul smells, telepathy regarding religious and moral matters, unexplained drops in temperature, distortions to the skin, face, body, or behavior, sudden immobility or immovability, levitation, and physical manifestations such as door slamming or breaking of furniture.[2] An entire battery of mental and physical symptoms, such as hallucinations, amnesia, and dizziness, can be added to the list.[3]

The exorcists described in this book make frequent use of these means to distinguish true possessions. A properly trained and experienced exorcist has many additional tricks in his bag. For example, a possessed person's aversion to holy water, blessed food, etc. is easy to fake, so the priest will use control groups. Not all the water used will be holy water, nor will all the objects be blessed, and so on.

---

[1] *The Roman Ritual of Exorcism*, Chapter One: "Instructions for Exorcising Those Possessed by Evil Spirit, no. 3.

[2] Malachi Martin, *Hostage to the Devil*, 13; this is the only time Malachi Martin will be cited in this text, due to the many controversies surrounding him, his work, and ideas.

[3] Fr. Jose Antonio Fortea, *Interview With an Exorcist: An Insider's Look at the Devil, Demonic Possession, and the Path to Deliverance*, 73.

The Roman Ritual of Exorcism provides many tips for the exorcists in its first chapter, such as No. 3 quoted above. The rest of Chapter One is provided in the Appendix.

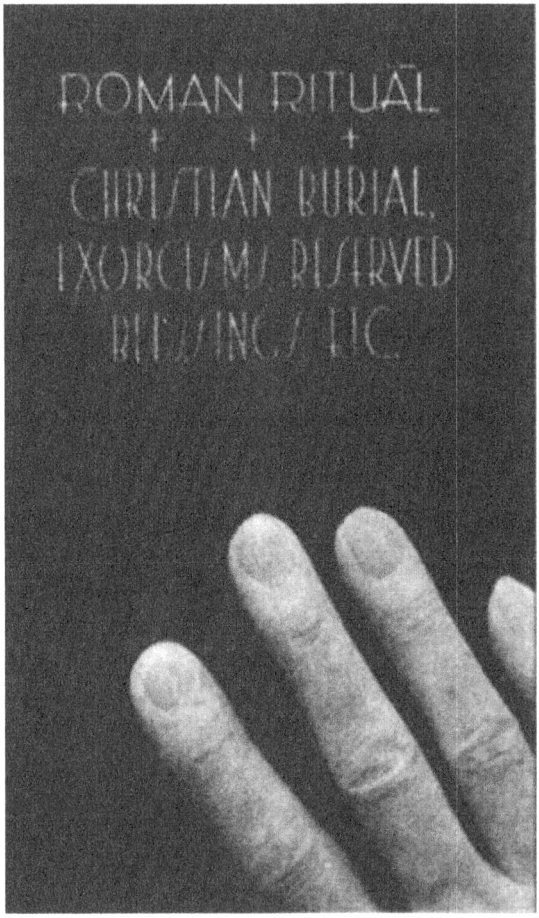

Figure 1: Roman Ritual for Exorcisms, from the St. Louis University, location of the 1949 exorcism which inspired the 1973 movie, *The Exorcist*. 1988 photo by Jerry Naunheim

You will notice many other important features to a valid, effective exorcism on display in the following accounts, such as the geographical requirement that the local bishop grant the exorcist permission to perform the rituals.

Geography is important. A priest is given power and dominion over any evil that wanders into his parish; the bishop or archbishop over his diocese; and the Pope over the entire world, since he is the steward to the King of Kings. You will notice how priests often struggle in the modern age to receive the permission of their local bishop.

Another common thread you will notice in the following accounts is the age of the possessed. All the people described in this book, it is believed, first suffered possession around the age of fourteen. It is not known why fourteen is such a vulnerable age – number-wise, you would think *thirteen* would be a more dangerous age.

Fourteen may be the age of possession because young people older than this receive the Sacrament of Confirmation, which is a great and indelible protection against the demonic. This is an imperfect theory, however, because Confirmation of sixteen and seventeen-year-olds is only a relatively recent custom. The possession of Nicola Aubrey, for example, occurred in 1565.

Regardless, take special care of children around the age of fourteen. Unfortunately, there are many ways to open the door to demonic influence.

The people described in this book were exposed to witchcraft, curses, and Ouija boards, all of which are extremely perilous.

I hope this book will have the effect of guarding your mind and soul against the devil. Think of it as sort of a vaccine or inoculation against evil. And, as instructed and provided at the very beginning of this book, frequently recite the Prayer to St. Michael while reading – at the beginning and close of each chapter or whenever frightened would be a good idea.

Emma Schmidt, 1926-28

If you're like me, you assumed that the green, pea soup vomit ejected by Regan in *The Exorcist* was just a Hollywood invention. Just more over-the-top theatrics, right? ... Right?

Unfortunately, no.

Figure 2: Rural Iowan children, c. 1926

The Exorcist movie and book was a composite of several different true exorcism stories. One case of exorcism had more impact than the others – that was the Mount Rainier case of

1949, which is the subject of the next chapter.

The exorcism that took place in sleepy Earling, Iowa in 1928, however, provided another detail, or perhaps "ingredient" is the better word.

The exorcism of Emma Schmidt is documented in several sources including Father Carl Vogl, a witness to the exorcism, in his 1936 German publication, *Satan Begone!*

NOTE: The full text of Father Vogl's booklet is included as an appendix to this book.

The principal exorcist, Father Theophilus Riesinger, himself wrote about the case in a 1934 book called *The Earling Possession case: An exposition of the exorcism of 'Mary', a demoniac*. Apart from the Father Vogl and Riesinger's booklets, there is also *The Devil Rocked Her Cradle* by David St. Clair.

You might also count a fourth book in this number, a novel at least partly inspired by this exorcism, William Peter Blatty's *The Exorcist*.

Earling, Iowa:
A Quiet Railroad Town

Though in Iowa, Shelby County was named for the first (and fifth) governor of Kentucky, Isaac Shelby. Shelby was called "Old Kings Mountain" for his defeat of the British at that location in the Revolutionary War.

The principal cities of Shelby County were founded by German Catholic immigrant families after the Civil War. That heritage left a lasting imprint on those cities, including Defiance, Panama, Portsmouth, Westphalia, and most notably Earling.

The soaring 150-foot-tall steeple of Earling's St. Joseph Catholic Church and a Franciscan convent are reminders of this lasting Catholic heritage, as well as a certain event involving a Franciscan priest.

Figure 3: Downtown Earling, Iowa, modern day

St. Joseph's Catholic Church and Parsonage, Earling
St. Boniface's Catholic Church, Westphalia
Catholic Parochial School, Westphalia
Catholic Church, Portsmouth
Catholic Church, Panama
Catholic Church, Defiance

Figure 4: The Catholic Churches of Shelby County, Iowa

Earling, Iowa has always been a quiet and small community. Even today, its population is just shy of 450 people. About an hour northeast of Omaha, Nebraska, Earling owes its existence as much to the railroad as the hard work of its German Catholic settlers. The city was first laid out in the 1880s when the Chicago, Milwaukee, & St. Paul Railway laid rail through the Iowa.

Apart from this, the history of Earling is unremarkable except for 23 days in 1928, when it briefly played host to the devil.

Witchcraft & Curses Open the Door

Emma Schmidt was born in 1882 and grew up in Marathon, Wisconsin before her family eventually settled in Earling.

Emma Schmidt is sometimes referred to as Anna Ecklund, as this is the pseudonym given to her by Father Carl Vogl, a witness to the exorcism, in his 1936 German publication, *Satan Begone!*

NOTE: The full text of Father Vogl's booklet is included as an appendix to this book.

Apart from the Father Vogl booklet, there is a second book, *The Devil Rocked Her Cradle* by David St. Clair. You might also count a third book in this number, a novel at least partly inspired by this exorcism, William Peter Blatty's *The Exorcist*.

As will be described below, the exorcism of Emma Schmidt was remarkable for the Hollywood-esque horror film episodes that occurred. One has to ask – **what terrible evil did this young woman commit to have such a horrific possession?**

In short, nothing. There is little indication why Emma Schmidt suffered such a possession in the midst of her devout life, except for a few significant allegations.

The Council Bluffs, Iowa *Daily Nonpareil* revisited the exorcism of Emma Schmidt in a 2003 article. It reported the following about the possibility of witchcraft being the triggering event for Schmidt's initial possession:

> Born in 1882, Schmidt's Aunt Mina was reputedly a witch "who had placed a spell on some herbs which she placed among the girl's food." [4] [5]

You might be thinking, what kind of aunt would do such a thing? A witch-kind of aunt, for one. Of course, Aunt Mina's actions might have been well-intentioned. Unfortunately for Emma Schmidt, it is impossible to accomplish good by doing evil. Attempting to do good with the assistance of witchcraft is an important example of this. Take heed. Whatever its guise, witchcraft is never benign.

During Emma Schmidt's later exorcism, the priest would question Schmidt's demonic possessors on this point. Not that you can trust the words of demons, but it is an interesting insight nonetheless:

Exorcist: "How long have you been torturing this poor woman?"

Devil: "Since her fourteenth year."

Exorcist: "How dared you enter into that innocent girl and torture her like that?"

Devil sneering: "Ha, did not her own father curse us

---

[4] "Earling site of last sanctioned exorcism," *The Daily Nonpareil*, 10/28/2003.

[5] Mina is described as one of Emma Schmidt's demonic possessors in Father Carl Vogl's account, *Begone Satan!*, "The Demon Jacob". As such, I believe the Daily Nonpareil's account of Mina is based on a basic misunderstanding. Father Vogl relates a conversation between the exorcist and Mina, in which Mina admitted to killing several children. This account might have been confused by the newspaper as relating to Emma Schmidt as a child.

into her?"[6]

When all was said and done, Emma Schmidt suffered possession from the age of fourteen to forty – over 26 years! Whatever happened during Schmidt's 14th year, whether it was the actions of her aunt, her father, or some other influence, Schmidt's behavior suddenly changed.
By all accounts, Emma Schmidt was a sincere girl, devoted to her Catholic faith and practicing it with dedication.[7] However, when she turned fourteen, she was suddenly repulsed by Holy Communion. She also expressed the desire to attack priests, destroy religious objects, and commit other sacrileges inside the church:

> There were times when she felt impelled to shatter her holy water font, when she could have attacked her spiritual adviser and could have suffocated him. Yes, there were suggestions urging her to tear down the very house of God.[8]

Though Schmidt wanted to continue attending Holy Mass, she felt as though something inside of her was preventing her from going, some "interior hidden power."
Schmidt's family took her to doctors, who could do nothing for her.
Eventually, they called in Father Theophilus Riesinger to perform the Rites of Exorcism.

---

[6] Father Carl Vogl, *Begone Satan!,* "One or More Devils"
[7] Emma Schmidt's story bears a striking resemblance to that of Anneliese Michel, whose story of heroic faith is told in a subsequent chapter.
[8] Father Carl Vogl, *Begone Satan!,* "The Lady in Question"

The Exorcist, Father Theophilus Riesinger

Theophilus Riesinger, O.F.M. Cap., belonged to the Capuchin Order of Friars. The Capuchins are one of the largest orders formed from the Franciscan Order. Friar Matteo da Bascio founded the Capuchins in 1525[9] as a return to the life of solitude and penance originally envisioned by St. Francis. You might also recognize the name "Capuchin," as a species of monkey so-named by Portuguese explorers for their resemblance to the brown-hooded Capuchin friars.

The name "Theophilus" is extremely interesting in context. The Gospel of Luke as well as the Acts of the Apostles, which Luke also wrote, are dedicated to "Theophilus". In Greek, *theophilus* simply means "lover of God."

Theophilus Xavier Riesinger was better known to parishioners as Father Theo.[10] Stout, with a dark heavy beard and wire spectacles, the Bavarian-born priest was originally assigned to two parishes in New York City. There, he began to answer requests to perform exorcisms. Unfortunately, local diocesan authorities may have been adverse to such heroics.

Exiled to Marathon, Wisconsin, Father Theophilus was assigned to a modest church called St. Anthony's. The ruggedness of the Capuchin Order made him an ideal fit for this rural assignment. He could easily transition from giving communion to wielding an ax to clear land for a new church building.

---

[9] Pope Clement VII approved of the Capuchin Order in 1528, and Friar Matteo was given permission to live as a hermit and to go about everywhere preaching to the poor, along with any who chose to follow him.

[10] Matthew Pearl, *Truly*Adventurous*, "The Exorcisms of Emma," which includes an author's note citing sources, but without more specificity, as follows: "The following story has been reported based on the firsthand accounts of those involved. Highly detailed notes on this case have been stored in a seminary library for many years and sealed with this message: 'These are not to be published through the press or from the pulpit.' The editorial team of Truly*Adventurous has reviewed these records, but we are among the few who ever have."

Figure 5: Father Theophilus Riesinger

As a twelve-year-old boy in Bavaria, Riesinger endured a long illness which later inspired his vocation to dedicate his life to God.[11] This experience prepared Riesinger for the austere life of a Capuchin. A fellow priest marveled at Riesinger's "superhuman" stamina, and another listed his qualities as including "nerves of steel and an iron constitution," as well as "a power-

---

[11] Pearl, Ibid.

ful, well-modulated voice, lively imagination, retentive memory."[12]

Notes from Riesinger's theology professors describe him as having "behavior always exemplary," "intellectual attainments gratifyingly successful," and "untiring diligence and inflexible energy."

Father Theophilus credited his practice of self-denial and ascetic prayer life as necessary for his work as an exorcist: "The priest who makes an exorcism must pray as he has never prayed before." "As a rule," he added, "priests who exorcise do not live more than a couple of years after an exorcism, but God has given me an extra gift of strength." Instead of "exorcising" he preferred simply calling his work "casting out devils."[13]

---

[12] Ibid.
[13] Ibid.

Describes Case of Earling Woman.

EXORCISM—

Widespread interest in the subject of exorcism has been aroused by the recent publication in pamphlet form and in several Catholic publications of the case of an Earling, Ia., woman who was freed of possession by evil spirits by a Wisconsin priest. This priest, Father Theophilus, exorcised the Iowa woman in 1926 and again in 1928.

Every Catholic priest when ordained is empowered to exorcise (to cast out devils), although he must have permission of his bishop in each case. Catholics are not required to believe in exorcisms, except those chronicled in the Scriptures.

A brief account of the exorcism of the Iowa woman by Father Theophilus was printed in Time magazine recently and reprinted in The Sunday Register, Feb. 16. The following interview with Father Theophilus is reprinted from The Milwaukee Journal.

The Exorcisms Begin

Father Theophilus' initial investigation of Emma Schmidt was conclusive. Emma responded violently when approached with blessed items, and only blessed items. As is typical in determining whether one is possessed, the exorcists will use a control group of unblessed items. Likewise, Emma Schmidt ate, but selectively refused to eat blessed food. Schmidt never saw the blessing take place, she simply knew what food was blessed and what was not.

Riesinger also discovered that the poorly educated Schmidt could speak Latin and German fluently. He explained this based on her exposure to those languages in church and in the German-settled Wisconsin and Iowa communities where she lived. Inexplicably, however, Schmidt could also speak Hebrew, Polish, and Italian.[14]

Father Theophilus determined that an exorcism was in order. After this initial 1926 exorcism, Schmidt's life regained some normalcy. This would not last long.

Father Theophilus was assigned in 1928 to St. Joseph Parish in Earling, Iowa. He requested permission from the local pastor, the appropriately-named Father Joseph Steiger, if he could bring Emma Schmidt to Earling for an exorcism. Theophilus hoped the distance would provide Emma with privacy. Father Joseph and the local ordinary, Thomas Drumm, Bishop of Des Moines, agreed, and preparations began at a local Franciscan convent.

Based on his preparations alone, this was not Father Theophilus' first exorcism. He instructed that Emma Schmidt be placed firmly upon the mattress of an iron bed at the Franciscan convent. Next, Emma's arm-sleeves and her dress were tightly bound so "as to prevent any devilish tricks." Father also selected only the strongest nuns to assist him. These precautions and the strength of the nuns were soon put to the test.

---

[14] Jason Offutt, "The Exorcism of Emma Schmidt," Mysterious Universe: 11/26/17.

The beginning of the exorcism triggered a horrific response from Emma Schmidt:

> Father Theophilus had hardly begun the formula of exorcism in the name of the Blessed Trinity, in the name of the Father, the Son, and the Holy Ghost, in the name of the Crucified Savior, when a hair-raising scene occurred. With lightning speed the possessed dislodged herself from her bed and from the hands of her guards; and her body, carried through the air, landed high above the door of the room and clung to the wall with a tenacious grip. All present were struck with a trembling fear. Father Theophilus alone kept his peace.[15]

Such compelling evidence of the supernatural! How would a skeptic explain this violation of gravity, except for group hysteria?

The nuns grabbed Schmidt and pulled her back down, all the while kicking and screaming, and re-tied her to the bed. Schmidt's body and face distorted in rage as she convulsed and howled.

After an extended period of refusing food, Emma Schmidt began to expel supernaturally copious amounts of "unusually foul smelling ... green vomit," according to the Daily Nonpareil.

Father Vogl described the "torrents" of vomit as follows:

> *You say torrents?* Actually those present had to live through some terrible experiences. It was heartrending to see all that came forth from the pitiable creature and often the ordeal was almost unbearable. Outpourings that would fill a pitcher, yes, even a pail, full of the most obnoxious stench were most unnatural. These came in quantities that were humanly speaking impossible to lodge in a normal being. At that the poor creature had

---

[15] Father Carl Vogl, *Begone Satan!*, "The Decisive Moment Had Arrived"

eaten scarcely anything for weeks, so that there had been reason to fear she would not survive. At one time the emission was a bowl full of matter resembling vomited macaroni. At another time an even greater measure, having the appearance of sliced and chewed tobacco leaves, was emitted. From ten to twenty times a day this wretched creature was forced to vomit though she had taken at the most only a tea-spoonful of water or milk by way of food.[16]

Literally, buckets of vomit after fasting *for weeks*. I don't know whether to laugh or cry.

Terrible voices and animal noises erupted endlessly from the woman's chest. Father Vogl describes a veritable parade of animals issuing forth from the woman:

This ugly bellowing and howling took place every day and at times it lasted for hours. At other times it sounded as though a horde of lions and hyenas were let loose, then again as the mewing of cats, the bellowing of cattle and the barking of dogs. A complete uproar of different animal noises would also resound. This was at first so taxing on the nerves of those present that the twelve nuns were forced to take turns at assisting in order to save themselves and to have the necessary strength to continue facing the siege.[17]

Can you imagine the poor nuns that were assisting the exorcist? Every one of their senses was being besieged: the smell of endless outpouring of filth and vomit, the sound of roaring lions, the sight of a woman defying gravity. One can only hope that the irrefutable signs of such powers and dominions had the opposite effect on their spiritual life, vivifying their faith lives – how great must God be, if He can overcome such evil?

---

[16] Vogl, Ibid.
[17] Father Vogl, *Begone Satan!*, "One or More Devils"

The weight of Emma Schmidt's body also fluctuated, as it twisted and writhed while tied the iron bed frame. At times, she became light enough to levitate, while also swelling at times, becoming heavy enough to bend the iron frame.

The Dramatic End

The demons possessing Emma Schmidt were eventually overpowered by God through the steadfastness of Father Theophilus. Theophilus eventually wrested the individual names out of the demons possessing Schmidt. Their voices bellowed out "Beelzebub, Judas, Jacob," and eventually the name of "Lucifer", himself, until they eventually fell silent.

Father Vogl described the final, dramatic moments of the wizened hero priest expelling the demons:

> It was on the twenty-third day of September, 1928, in the evening about nine o'clock that, with a sudden jerk of lightning speed the possessed woman broke from the grip of her protectors and stood erect before them. Only her heels were touching the bed. At first sight it appeared as if she were to be hurled up to the ceiling. "Pull her down! Pull her down" called the pastor while Father [Theophilus] blessed her with the relic of the cross, saying: **"Depart ye fiends of hell! Begone Satan, the Lion of Judah reigns!"**
>
> At that very moment the stiffness of the woman's body gave way and she fell upon the bed. Then a piercing sound filled the room causing all to tremble vehemently. Voices saying, "Beelzebub, Judas, Jacob, Mina," could be heard. And this was repeated over and over until they faded far away into the distance.
>
> "Beelzebub, Judas, Jacob, Mina." To these words were added: "Hell ... hell ... hell!
>
> Everyone present was terrified by this gruesome scene. It was the long awaited sign indicating that Satan was

forced to leave his victim at last and to return to hell with his associates.

Father Theophilus final words to Emma's possessors became the title of Father Carl Vogl's account of the exorcism.

Emma Schmidt was next described as finally opening her eyes, which had been impossible during the exorcism sessions, and smiling.

The exorcism had lasted 23 days.

Roland Doe,[18] 1949

The exorcism which *re*-captured the nation's imagination – this is the exorcism which inspired William Peter Blatty's 1971 horror novel turned movie, *The Exorcist*. Blatty, himself, heard rumors of the exorcism from the Jesuits priests of Georgetown University, while a student there as a member of the class of 1950.

Between 1950 and 1971, many priests had begun dismissing the reality of the demonic, including many Jesuits. Merely metaphorical or social evil was preached from the pulpit. The Devil was just a personification of the evil within us. Demons did not exist. Psychologists and academics, even to this day, dismissed all supernatural phenomena as superstitious nonsense.

This is why *The Exorcist* re-captured the nation's imagination. The Devil had succeeded, for a time, in convincing the world he did not exist.

Michael Cuneo discusses *The Exorcist* case at length in the opening chapter of his book *American Exorcism*. Cuneo points out that the case was sensationalized. Some of the story's most basic details were changed. For example, the possessed child was a boy who lived in Mount Rainier, not a girl living in an upscale Georgetown neighborhood.

The Georgetown setting was due to the author's personal encounter with the story while attending Georgetown University. Blatty's time at Georgetown clearly made a lifelong impact: "Those years at Georgetown were probably the best years of

---

[18] Ronald Edwin Hunkeler was given the pseudonym, Roland Doe, by the original Washington, DC newspaper accounts of the possession in 1949.

my life," Blatty said in a 2015 interview. "Until then, I'd never had a home."[19]

Projectile pea soup vomit and spinning heads were just literary embellishments. Once you hear the true story, however, you will wonder why any embellishment was needed in the first place.

Note: Unfortunately, the ridiculous quantities of green, projectile vomit were not merely embellishments. Check out the previous chapter detailing the exorcism of Emma Schmidt.

---

[19] "William Peter Blatty, Author of 'The Exorcist', Dies at 89," *The Washington Post*, January 13, 2017.

The Impact of *The Exorcist*

The Exorcist case is important not only because of the extreme supernatural phenomenon on display. It's important for the impact it had on the American psyche. It is the single most familiar exorcism to the wider American public, whether or not people realize it was based on a true story.[20]

The Exorcist left an indelible impression on the world's imagination more so than any other case of possession ever has. This is because it was thrust upon the world after several decades of mounting disbelief in the existence of Satan.

Although *The Exeter Report* showed that fear of Satan was already on the rise in England, exorcisms in America had declined precipitously. The United States had fallen into a deep sleep after its victory over evil during World War II. Even the Pentecostals had tried to dampen their more charismatic deliverances.[21]

The launch of *The Exorcist* in movie theaters all over America released a flood of repressed fears. It had been simple enough for the Devil to recede into the background of a world faced with nuclear annihilation and extinction. Then came the *The Exorcist*, and an ancient history of satanic awareness surged to the foreground. Many people found themselves unable to cope with the sudden jolt of religious revival, or at least the reminder of supernatural realities.

This resurgence in satanic awareness resulted in thousands of people suddenly fearing that they or a loved one was possessed. Father Tom Bermingham, one of the film's minor actors and a researcher for Blatty's book, suddenly found himself swarmed by hundreds of requests from individuals seeking an exorcism.[22] Exorcism and possession suddenly became mainstream, and the devil who had benefitted from being ignored

---

[20] Jamie H. Parsons, *The Manifest Darkness: Exorcism and Possession in the Christian Tradition*, 2012, 64-68.

[21] W. Scott Poole, *Satan in America*, 112.

[22] Michael Cuneo, *American Exorcism: Expelling Demons in the Land of Plen-

and forgotten, now was suddenly benefitting from being a celebrity.

Not Mount Rainier

For one thirteen-year-old boy,[23] Satan had been a reality, long before the sale of the movie rights.
First off, let's get the location right.
Roland Doe, the pseudonym used for the possessed boy, is commonly described as being a resident of Mount Rainier, Maryland. At the time of the first exorcisms in 1949, Mount Rainier was a small, working-class community of nearly 8,000 residents quietly tucked away in Victorian homes and bungalows on the outskirts of Washington, D.C.

Ever since the early 1980s and the release of (the first) *Exorcist* movie, local teens have been flocking to a then-vacant lot at the corner of Bunker Hill Road and 33rd Street in the residential heart of Mount Rainier.[24] An urban legend, spawned by local newspapers, holds that this was the former site of the house of Roland Doe.[25] Prince George's County teens have long delighted in roaming the lot at all hours of the night, drinking beer, conducting initiations, erecting wooden crosses

---

ty, 12.

[23] Roland Doe is often described as being fourteen; however, his birthdate has been confirmed as June 1, 1935 making him thirteen at the time of the first exorcism. Also, it is interesting that both Roland Doe and Emma Schmidt first suffered possession at approximately the same age.

[24] Though 3210 Bunker Hill Road is commonly listed as the home of the Doe family, research conducted by Mark Opsasnick of *Strange Magazine* concluded that the family's actual address was 3807 40th Avenue, Cottage City, Maryland. Opsasnick found that the yearbook entries for the graduating seniors of Gonzaga High School listed their home addresses. Based on the convergence of other clues including the boy's birthdate, Opsasnick believes he found the correct entry for Roland Doe. A copy of the yearbook page is provided at the end of this chapter.

[25] Mark Opsasnick, "The Haunted Boy of Cottage City: The Cold Hard Facts Behind the Story That Inspired 'The Exorcist'", *Strange Magazine*, Issue 20 (1999).

on the property, and yelling and screaming until local police are forced to come and chase them away.

Along with several other sources, Dean Landolt, a lifelong Mount Rainier resident of over seventy years, informed researchers that, "I was very good friends with Father Hughes, the priest involved in that case, as was my brother Herbert. Father Hughes told me two things: one was that the boy lived in Cottage City, and the other is that he went on to graduate from Gonzaga High and turned out fine."[26]

It's easy to understand the confusion. Cottage City is an even smaller, semi-isolated community just a short distance from Mount Rainier. Cottage City is nestled between the towns of Colmar Manor and Brentwood.

Figure 6: DO NOT use Ouija Boards. Terrible idea.

---

[26] Opsasnick, ibid.

Don't Play With Ouija Boards

Hollywood's decision to sensationalize the story does not mean the source exorcism of Roland Doe was without bizarre phenomena.

In a 1979 article for *Fate* magazine, Steve Erdmann includes the following description of events taken from a diary maintained by one of the priest-exorcists, Father Bishop: [27] [28]

> January 15, 1949—A dripping noise was heard in his grandmother's bedroom by the boy and his grandmother. A picture of Christ on the wall shook and scratching noises were heard under the floor boards. From that night on scratching was heard every night from 7 p.m. until midnight. This continued for ten consecutive days. After three days of silence, the boy heard nighttime "squeaking shoes" on his bed that continued for six consecutive nights.

And in another description: [29]

> For some time prior to the exorcism [...] the unidentified boy had been tormented by a battery of bizarre phenomena: There were scratchings and rappings on his bedroom walls, pieces of fruit and other objects were sent flying in

---

[27] Steve Erdmann, "The Truth Behind The Exorcist," *Fate* Magazine, January 1975; "Aunt Tillie" referred to elsewhere as "Aunt Harriet".

[28] The diary was entitled "Case Study by Jesuit Priests." Erdmann describes the origin and chain of title for this diary: during the fall of 1949 an unnamed Georgetown University student, whose father was a psychiatrist at St. Elizabeth's Hospital in Washington, D.C. and may have been involved in the case, told Georgetown faculty member Father Eugene B. Gallagher, S.J., of the existence of the mysterious diary. Father Gallagher obtained from the psychiatrist a 16-page diary-like document written as a guide for future exorcisms. Mark Opsasnick states in his piece for *Strange Magazine*, referenced many times herein, that the diary was kept and written by Father Bishop.

[29] Michael Cuneo, *American Exorcism: Expelling Demons in the Land of Plenty* (New York: Doubleday, 2001), 5.

his presence, and his bed mysteriously gyrated across the floor while he tried to sleep.

Why were these things happening to the pseudonymously named Roland Doe? Was it just random? No, it appears the child's aunt introduced him to the demonic.

Roland Doe was born into a German Lutheran family and was his parent's only child. Since there were no other children in the family, Roland looked to his parents and other adults in his household for playmates. The boy spent much of his time with his Aunt Tillie.[30] Tillie was reportedly a "spiritualist", which seems to indicate that she dabbled in witchcraft and other occult interests. She introduced Roland to the Ouija board.[31] This is when the trouble began.

A very detailed diary was kept by one of the priests that would later exorcise Roland. Under the heading January 26, 1949, the diary records the following concerning Aunt Tillie:[32]

"Aunt Tillie," who had a deep interest in spiritualism and had introduced Roland to the Ouija Board, died of multiple sclerosis at the age of 54. Mrs. Doe suspected there may have been some connection between her death and the seemingly strange events that continued to take place. At one point during the manifestations Mrs. Doe asked, "If you are Tillie, knock three times." Waves of air began striking the grandmother, Mrs. Doe, and Roland and three knocks were heard on the floor. Mrs. Doe again queried, "If you are Tillie, tell me positively by knocking four times." Four knocks were heard, followed by claw scratchings on Roland's mattress.

---

[30] Steve Erdmann, "The Truth Behind The Exorcist," *Fate* Magazine, January 1975; "Aunt Tillie" referred to elsewhere as "Aunt Harriet".

[31] Thomas B. Allen, *Possessed: The True Story of an Exorcism*, Book Country, 11 November 2013.

[32] Erdmann, ibid.

Mrs. Doe also recounted using blessed candles when a comb flew across the room and extinguished them.[33] Other observations include fruit flying across the room, a kitchen table turning over, milk and food moving off a table, a coat and hanger flying across the room, a Bible landing at Roland's feet, and a rocker spinning around while Roland was sitting in it. Roland was also removed from school after his desk moved around the classroom floor on its own.[34]

The desk event left an indelible impression on one eyewitness. Roland's best childhood friend also recounted this event in detail in a 1998 interview with Mark Opsasnick:

> One thing happened regarding all of this and I have a hard time clearing it in my mind. We were in eighth grade, it was the '48-'49 school year and we were in a class together at Bladensburg Junior High. He was sitting in a chair and it was one of those deals with one arm attached and it looked like he was shaking the desk—the desk was shaking and vibrating extremely fast and I remember the teacher yelling at him to stop it and I remember he kind of yelled "I'm not doing it" and they took him out of class and that was the last I ever saw of him in school. The desk certainly did not move around the room like that book [*Possessed*] said, it was just shaking. I don't know if he was doing it or what was doing it because I just can't clear it in my mind.

The diary also describes Mrs. Doe taking a bottle of holy water and sprinkling its contents throughout the house. When she returned the bottle to its shelf, it flew across the room on its own but did not break.[35]

Another night, while holding a lit blessed candle at Roland's bedside, Mrs. Doe experienced the whole bed rocking back and forth.

---

[33] Erdmann, ibid.
[34] Erdmann, ibid.
[35] Erdmann, ibid.

The Need for a Priest

According to *American Exorcism* by Michael Cuneo, the boy's family initially requested the help of a Protestant minister, Luther Miles Schulze, but this only worsened the situation.

Pastor Schulze had long been interested in parapsychology, and arranged for the boy to spend the night of February 17, 1949 in his home for observation.[36] Schulze witnessed several disturbing phenomenon during this and subsequent encounters, including household objects and furniture moving by themselves.

Bill Brinkley interviewed Pastor Schulz for an article for *The Washington Post* entitled "Pastor Tells Eerie Tale of 'Haunted' Boy".[37] Schulz describes the as boy sleeping nearby in a twin bed. In the dark, the minister reported hearing vibrating sounds from the bed and scratching sounds on the wall. Schulz also observed the boy sitting in a heavy armchair, which tilted on its

---

[36] Allen, ibid.
[37] *The Washington Post*, August 10, 1949.

own and tipped over. While the boy was laying on them, a pallet of blankets also inexplicably moved around the room.[38]

Schulze soon advised the boy's parents to "see a Catholic priest."[39] The family then sought help from the local Jesuit community. Despite their theological disagreements with the Catholic Church, Protestants generally acknowledge that priests are needed for the most difficult possessions.

Any ordained priest, with the blessing and permission of the local bishop, can perform an exorcism. Exorcisms, for that matter, are not all that rare. Elements of exorcisms are (or were once) incorporated into many Catholic liturgies, including the Mass and the Rite of Baptism, for example.

Figure 7: Father Gabriele Amorth,
the foremost Catholic exorcist priest (now deceased)

---

[38] *The Evening Star*, another Washington, D.C. paper, wrote a story of its own on the incident, which was published on the same date, August 10, 1949. This article originally named the boy's parents "Mr. and Mrs. John Doe" and the boy, "Roland".

[39] Allen, ibid.

Nevertheless, the Church provides training for priests who are asked to specialize in exorcisms. This process is described by Father Gabriele Amorth, the designated exorcist for the Diocese of Rome, in his book, *An Exorcist Tells His Story*. Father Amorth describes the benefit of special training:

> We cannot improvise an exorcism. To assign such a task to any priest is like demanding that someone perform surgery after reading a textbook on the subject. Many, too many, things are not written in a text but are learned only through experience.[40]

Father Amorth also laments the decline of "the school" for training exorcists:

> I am convinced that allowing the ministry of exorcism to die is an unforgiveable deficiency to be laid squarely at the door of bishops… Today the exorcist is seen as a rarity, almost impossible to find… The Catholic hierarchy must say a forceful *mea culpa*. As a result of this negligence, we now have lost what once was the school; in the past, a practicing exorcist would instruct a novice.[41]

---

[40] Gabriele Amorth, *An Exorcist Tell His Story*, Ignatius Press, 1999, 68.
[41] Amorth, 55.

The First Exorcist: Father Edward Hughes

Father Edward Albert Hughes (1918-1980) was a Catholic priest who served as an assistant pastor from June 16, 1948 to June 18, 1960 at St. James Church in Mt. Rainier, Maryland. Father Hughes performed the first round of exorcisms on Roland Doe.

Just as Mrs. Doe had before him, Father Hughes is described as experiencing supernatural events concerning blessed objects:[42]

> Hughes reported giving a bottle of holy water and candles to Roland's parents to give to Roland before he went to sleep. The parents said the telephone table on which the holy water sat smashed into hundreds of pieces while the candle flamed up, torching the ceiling.

Shortly thereafter, it is recorded that Father Hughes received permission to exorcise the boy and the ritual was undertaken first and unsuccessfully at Georgetown University Hospital

As discussed before, it is imperative that the local Bishop grant permission and authority to the presiding priest. It is not certain whether Father Hughes received such permission. This may be the reason Father Hughes was ultimately unsuccessful in exorcising Roland Doe. Father Hughes also only had a short time with the boy, and may have only attempted an abbreviated or informal exorcism.

The next attempt at exorcism would occur when the Doe family left Maryland for Missouri.

---

[42] Allen, ibid.

The Exorcisms

The priests who initially handled the case were not trained exorcists, so they took various precautions. They ensured that the child underwent a battery of medical and psychiatric evaluations and was placed under 24-hour observation.

Dr. J. B. Rhine, director of the Parapsychology Laboratory at Duke University, reportedly described the phenomena associated with the possession, the "most impressive manifestation he has heard of in the poltergeist field."[43]

Despite the best help of medical professionals, the situation continued to deteriorate:

> When a natural cure wasn't found for his affliction, [...] and the bizarre symptoms threatened to rage completely out of control, it was decided to pursue a more drastic course of action. A Jesuit priest in his fifties was assigned to the case, and over the next several weeks [...] he performed more than twenty exorcisms on the boy. In all but the last of these, [according to an article in the *Post*] the boy broke into a violent tantrum of screaming, cursing and voicing of Latin phrases—a language he had never studied—whenever the priest reached those climactic points of the 27-page [exorcism] ritual in which commanded the demon to depart. It was the last of the exorcisms, after two nerve-jangling months, that finally did the trick. Following its completion, the strange symptoms disappeared entirely, and the boy was restored to full health.[44]

One of the attending priests kept a meticulous diary during the boy's exorcism. This diary was obtained by Blatty while he was researching *The Exorcist* and served as a major inspiration

---

[43] "Minister Tells Parapsychologists Noisy 'Ghost' Plagued Family," *The Evening Star*, August 10, 1949.
[44] Cuneo, 6.

for the novel. The diary details many of the supernatural phenomena that occurred during the exorcisms.

Many of the phenomena associated with demonic possessions can be attributed to mental illness, even some of the amazing displays of seemingly superhuman strength. The following, however, cannot be attributed to merely natural causes.

The exorcist's diary described mysterious brandings and inflammations that spontaneously materialized on the thirteen-year-old boy's skin at various points during the ordeal. The brandings were not just random shapes. The brandings sometimes formed entire words, such as the word "SPITE". There were times when images, even portraits, formed on the boy's skin, including a hideous satanic visage.

The diary also described furniture shaking and crashing in the boy's presence. There was also one particularly memorable incident in which a hospital nightstand flung itself from floor to ceiling.[45]

Perhaps some might dismiss such witness testimony out of hand, since it is coming from religious men. Men of faith are prone to delusions, right? Ignore the fact that Jesuit priests are among the most educated people in the world, and have been for the last five centuries.

However, these incidents were not just witnessed by the exorcist priests. Cuneo notes that these incidents were also witnessed by a physics professor from Washington University. The professor later remarked that there is much we have yet to discover concerning the nature of electromagnetism.[46] Truly.

---

[45] Cuneo, 7.
[46] Ibid.

Figure 8: *The Exorcist* movie still, "... an old priest and a young priest", as potrayed by Max Von Sydow and Jason Miller, respectively

The Second Round of Exorcisms: An Old Priest & a Young Priest

Father Raymond J. Bishop, S.J. was a Jesuit priest who assigned to teach at St. Louis University. In case you are wondering, no – Father Bishop never became Bishop Bishop. He spent the last 20 years of his life teaching at another Jesuit institution, Creighton University in Nebraska.

Sometime in March 1949, Father Bishop was approached by one of his female students. She asked for the priest's help with her thirteen-year-old cousin, Roland Doe (at this point, sometimes also referred to by a second pseudonym, Robbie Manheim). After contacting his close friend, Father William Sporing Bowdern, the two priests decided to perform the boy's exorcism together.[47][48]

Father Bowdern was the pastor of St. Francis Xavier Church, the church located on the grounds of St. Louis Uni-

---

[47] Troy Taylor, *The Devil Came to St. Louis: The True Story of the 1949 Exorcism*, Whitechapel Productions Press: 2006.

[48] Steven A. LaChance, *Confrontation with Evil: An In-Depth Review of the 1949 Possession that Inspired* The Exorcist, Llewellyn Worldwide: 2017.

versity. In addition to the permission of the local bishop, the assistance of the priest with authority over the local geographical area would be crucial to the success of the exorcism.

The age difference between the two Jesuit priests, Father Bishop and Father Bowdern, was not as well defined as *The Exorcist* movie portrayed it. Bowdern was 52 and Bishop, his assistant, was 43.

According to the diary, Father Bishop met the boy for the first time on March 9, 1949, and witnessed the scratches on the boy's body and the unexplained movements of his mattress.

Three days later, on March 11,[49] Father Bowdern arrived on the scene. After Roland fell asleep around 11pm, Bowdern and Bishop began praying a Novena for the intercession of St. Francis Xavier. Bowdern also blessed the boy with a first class relic of St. Francis Xavier,[50] and fixed a relic-encrusted crucifix under the boy's pillow. Shortly thereafter, both priests departed and the boy's relatives left his room.

Figure 9: Father William Bowdern

---

[49] Opsasnick, ibid.
[50] This particular relic was a piece of bone from the forearm of St. Francis Xavier.

After only a short time had passed, a loud noise was heard in Roland's room and the five relatives present rushed back to the boy's bedroom. They discovered that a large book case had moved, a bench had been turned over, and the crucifix had been moved to the edge of the bed. The shaking of Roland's mattress had also resumed and only came to a halt after family members yelled, "Aunt Tillie, stop!"

The exorcism began on March 16 after Father Bowdern received the permission of the local bishop, Archbishop Joseph E. Ritter, to begin the formal rite of exorcism.

That night Father Bowdern was again accompanied by Father Bishop, as well as a Jesuit scholastic,[51] Walter Halloran. A series of exorcisms would occur over the next months and into April. During this time, the ritual was performed at various locations including the boy's aunt's house in Normandy, Missouri,[52] the nearby rectory (likely of St. Francis Xavier parish), and the Alexian Brothers Hospital in the southern section of St. Louis.[53]

---

[51] A scholastic is the stage in a Jesuit's career after novice, i.e. after they have graduated from the novitiate. Scholastics are not yet ordained priests. A Jesuit seminarian typically attends university as a scholastic, and this occurs in the third through fifth or sixth year of being a Jesuit.

[52] This is a different aunt from Roland Doe's Aunt Harriet or "Tillie".

[53] Erdmann describes that on one occasion Roland got his hand on a bedspring, broke it off, and jabbed it into a priest's arm. It is uncertain whether

Figure 10: Father Walter Halloran, then just a Jesuit Scholastic and not yet a priest

He Is Gone

Finally, on April 18, 1949, the nightmare came to an end.[54] The precise number of exorcisms performed is not known for certain, but the number likely exceeded twenty, as is typical of the exorcisms described in this book.

Late in the night, Father Bowdern succeeded in forcing Roland to wear a chain of holy medals and to hold a crucifix in his hands. Roland's demeanor visibly softened, and he calmly asked questions about the meanings of certain Latin prayers.

Bowdern continued the ritual and demanded to know the name of the demon that was possessing Roland and when he would leave the boy. Roland erupted into a tantrum, but nevertheless admitted that he was one of the fallen angels.

Bowdern persisted with the ritual until 11:00 p.m., at which point Roland interrupted the priest. There was a new voice coming from the boy. The voice announced himself as St. Michael. St. Michael roared through Roland the following command:

> Satan! Satan! I am St. Michael! I command you, Satan, and the other evil spirits to leave this body, in the name of Dominus, immediately! Now! Now! *Now!*

Roland's body shook with one last spasm before falling quiet. "He is gone," Roland announced.

Roland would later tell Father Bowdern that he had experienced a vision of St. Michael holding a flaming sword. Twelve days later Roland and his family left Missouri and returned to Maryland.

By all accounts, Roland Doe, or Ronald Edwin Hunkeler, his real name, lived the rest of his life in peace, in the most ordinary of ways. Doe/Hunkeler graduated from Gonzaga High

---

[54] Opsasnick, ibid.

School in 1954 and, it seems, played a lot of canasta with friends and family.

Family friends had little else of note to say about the boy or his family, except one notable change occurred following the boy's successful exorcism by Fathers Bowdern and Bishop. They converted to Catholicism.[55]

Figure 11: Ronald Edwin Hunkeler, the real Roland Doe, yearbook page, graduating senior class 1954, Gonzaga High School

---

[55] Opsasnick uncovered this detail in his interviews of the Does' neighbors in Cottage City. Alvin Kagey, a childhood friend of Roland and now a dentist in Southern Virginia, provided this detail.

Anneliese Michel, 1976

In 1976, the exorcism of a young German woman began which would continue through 67 grueling rites of exorcism. The truly unique part of this story is that the woman consented to the torture of demonic possession for salvation of souls. Her heroic story of sacrifice would later inspire the movie *The Exorcism of Emily Rose*. Tragically, Anneliese Michel made the ultimate sacrifice and ultimately did not survive the exorcism.

Anneliese's death triggered a court case that stunned the world. Her parents and the two priests who ministered to her were accused of negligent homicide.

Today, many consider her a saint, and her sacrifice is venerated around the world. Here is her extraordinary story.[56]

A Devout Young Catholic

Anneliese was born on September 21, 1952 in Klingenberg, Germany. Klingensberg, which translates as "Blade Mountain," is a small town overlooking the Main River and the ancient forests of Oldenwald and Spessart. Anneliese and her three sisters were raised in a devout Catholic family. Her father Josef had considered entering the priesthood, and three of her aunts were nuns.

---

[56] *from* The Occult Museum, "A Soul Possessed: The True Story of the Exorcism of Anneliese Michel," 4/26/2016.

By the time Anneliese was a teenager, she had discerned a career as a catechist, teaching young children about the Catholic faith and theology. Anneliese describes this in letters she wrote to her mother, Anna:

"... I had come to the resolution, not to pursue the Abitur, but to become a catechist. ... There are no accidents in life. It is all in the providence of God. So I have arranged things with the Mother of God that I will become a catechist ..."[57]

Anneliese exhibited a maturity and desire for self-sacrifice well beyond her years. She was acutely aware of the suffering of the poor of the world.

Figure 12: Anneliese in her school days

She wrote the following while still in the German equivalent of high school:

---

[57] Uwe Wolff, *Der Teufel is in Mir*, p. 99.

> "Actually, I am quite glad I have been sick, since one comes to see things. One comes to recognize that there are other values besides money, riches and cars, which are worth living for; that one is on this earth for the glory of God and not for transitory things. You should consider this also sometimes. When one is healthy and is immersed in his daily routine, he thinks, all is well with me, why should I be concerned if others in Biafra or Latin America are starving to death, the important thing is that all is going well with me. What is worse at the present time is the indifference towards our neighbors... People today can be so inhuman because all is going well for them. Really, the horrors of the last war ought to remain imprinted on them. But today that is all forgotten."[58]

Anneliese was a woman of great compassion and devotion. It is little wonder that she would accept the opportunity to offer her life for the salvation of souls. She wrote openly of such martyrdom:

> "You can mark one thing for sure, I want to go to heaven, cost what it may; to gain heaven, nothing is too much for me...On that account I should place my life at the disposal of others out of love for God, and hope more for the reward of God than for the reward of men. Better to be despised by men than by God."[59]

While in her early 20s, Anneliese had a vision of the Virgin Mary. Our Lady asked her if she was prepared to suffer much for German youth and priests. Anneliese agreed. The suffering would be in the form of demonic possession. She was to be a "victim soul." By her sacrifice, Anneliese was to show Germany and the world that devils really do exist. Throughout her possession, she still attended Holy Mass, prayed the Rosary,

---

[58] Ibid. 100-101.
[59] Ibid.

and received the Sacraments.

Certain changes were introduced to the Holy Mass during Anneliese's life. For example, for the first time in the history of the Catholic Church, lay people were permitted to receive Holy Communion in their hands, as opposed to on the tongue. Anneliese instinctively felt this was wrong, and found a parish that had not adopted this practice.

Many clergy during this time also ceased believing in the existence of Satan and demons, opting instead for a metaphorical understanding of evil. Many clergy were also openly rebelling against Paul VI's papal encyclical *Humanae Vitae* (1968), which re-asserted the Church's rejection of contraception.

Figure 13: The Michel Family, Anneliese is pictured on the left, standing

The Torments Begin

Anneliese's sufferings began in 1968, the same year Pope Paul VI issued *Humanae Vitae*. Around her sixteenth birthday, Anneliese suddenly lost consciousness. She dismissed the episode, but that same night she was awakened around midnight. An invisible force was pinning her down and pressing against her stomach. She tried to yell to her sister in the bed next to her, but found her tongue, too, was paralyzed.[60] The incident was forgotten until the following August 1969. She again experienced paralysis, unable to move her arms, speak, or even breathe. The next morning, Anneliese's parents brought her to their family physician, Dr. Gerhard Vogt, who quickly referred them to the neurologist, Dr. Luthy.

She was 17 and began to suffer from convulsions. After treatment at the Wurzburg Psychiatric Clinic, she was diagnosed with epilepsy and grand mal seizures.

Soon after, Anneliese started experiencing hallucinations while praying. She described these to Dr. Luthy in September 1973 as *Fratzen* or "ghastly demonic faces." Anneliese told him she saw these faces often and that the devil was in her.

Anneliese visited Dr. Vogt and an ear specialist in the spring of 1972 after hearing an incessant knocking in her bedroom. Rapping sounds were coming from inside the closet, under the floor boards, and along the ceiling. It was confirmed that she suffered from no hearing problems, as well that her sisters were hearing the same sounds.

Anneliese also relayed to Dr. Lenner in the fall of 1973 that she was assaulted by terrible stenches, which she likened to burning fecal matter.[61] At this point, only Anneliese smelled these stenches.

Anneliese described her torment in a conversation recorded by Father Renz on February 1, 1976:

> "It was especially gruesome at the time of the Abitur. Oh, Herr Pater, you cannot imagine that most awful dread (*grausen*). It is a terror which goes through all my limbs and settles there. It is a dread that makes you think that you are right there, in the middle of hell. You are totally, utterly de-

---

[60] Father Jose Fortea, *Anneliese Michel: A True Story of a Case of Demonic Possession, Germany – 1976*, chapter 2: "First Encounters".
[61] Ibid. Ch. 3.

serted. You can call all you want for help, to the Mother of God maybe, but they are all deaf. I think that is how it must have been for our Savior on the Mount of Olives, where they say he was beset by the shudders of death. Although I think for him it must have been worse, for, after all he had taken all the sins of the people on himself, all the sins of the world."[62]

Understandably, Anneliese likens her torments to Jesus' Agony in the Garden.

During the following months, her mental state deteriorated into increasingly erratic behavior. She began to eat flies, spiders and coal. She even bit off the head of a dead bird. In one instance, she crawled under a table and barked like a dog for two days. She could be heard screaming through the walls of her bedroom for hours on end. Tearing off her clothes and urinating on the floor became a regular occurrence.

In 1975, Anneliese's parents finally gave up on psychiatric treatment. Instead, they looked to the Church for healing. An exorcist from a nearby town examined Anneliese and concluded that she was indeed demonically possessed. After two failed requests, the local Bishop finally granted permission[63] to administer the Rite of Exorcism.

The Shrine at San Damiano

Monika Fichtel roomed with Anneliese for most of her stay in Mittelberg college and remembered Anneliese as joyful and positive, rarely, if ever, discussing her health concerns. In later correspondence with Monika, Anneliese encouraged her to pray and suggested she obtain holy water from San Damiano, Italy. Anneliese was very devoted to

---

[62] Dr. Felicitas D. Goodman, *The Exorcism of Anneliese Michel*, Doubleday & Co., Inc., Garden City, New York, 1981, p. 32.

[63] Some sources report that the two priests which performed the exorcisms were neither supported nor assigned by the local bishop. However,

and often visited the Marian shrine of "Our Lady of the Roses" at San Damiano, where the Virgin Mary is said to have appeared to Rosa Quattrini.

Despite such devotion, Anneliese's mother related to her father Josef that she had witnessed her daughter standing before their statue of the Virgin Mary with her face twisted in hatred and jet black eyes.

In the fall of 1973, Anneliese's father Josef took the family on a pilgrimage to San Damiano, which had been arranged by family friend Thea Hein. The following account of their pilgrimage comes from an interview with Hein.[64]

Figure 14: Photograph taken during an apparition of the Blessed Virgin

---

[64] Fr. Fortea, translated telephone conversation between Lawrence LeBlanc and Thea Hein, September 2006.

Mary at San Damiano on December 8, 1967, Feast of the Immaculate Conception

When the family arrived in San Damiano, Anneliese was unable to enter the shrine. She said that the soil burned her feet like fire. She tried to enter the shrine from around the back, but again could not get past the garden. The shrine's holy pictures and sacramentals were also too painful for Anneliese to look at.

Pilgrims to the San Damiano shrine drink from a miraculous well. Thea repeatedly offered Anneliese water from the well, but she refused overcome by its stench. Anneliese also refused to wear a holy medal that Josef bought for her. She claimed it weighed heavily against her chest, suffocating her. Anneliese also tore off a medal worn by Thea by grabbing at her dress. Anneliese later knocked Thea down on the bus, breaking her rosary.

On the way home, Anneliese's behavior was still disturbed. She attacked Thea with crude language and spoke in a deep voice like a man. Anneliese also exuded a stench, like burning fecal matter. This time, everyone on the bus could smell the stench.

Figure 15: Father Arnold Renz

The Exorcists

The Church assigned Fathers Arnold Renz and Ernst Alt to exorcise Anneliese Michel.

Wilhelm "Arnold" Renz was born in 1911 in Hiltensweiler in southern Germany. Ordained in 1938, Father Renz's first priestly assignment was as a missionary in Shaowu, China. He would remain in China throughout World War II until he was expelled by the Communists in 1952.

In 1965, Father Renz was named superior of a monastery and parish in Ruck-Schippach funded by German mystic, prophet, and third order Franciscan Barbara Weigand. In May 1898, the Blessed Mother reportedly told Barbara at the dawning of the 20th century that the coming century would be "quite a bad time": "Mankind stands trembling in fully anxious expectation before the days of the future."[65] Weigand founded the Eucharistic League of Love.

Father Ernst Alt was born in 1937 in Eppelborn, Germany. He was a member of an order of priest-missionaries called the Montfort Fathers. They were named after St. Louis de Montfort, whose *True Devotion to Mary* has inspired centuries of Catholics consecrated themselves to Jesus through Mary.

Due to organizational problems within the Montfort Fathers, Father Alt was eventually reassigned to a parish as a Diocesan priest, the Diocese of Wurzburg.

Father Alt's connection to Anneliese's case appears not to be coincidental. Alt describes spiritual pre-cognition of Anneliese's possession. He also describes an invisible assault on his person while celebrating the Mass, as if he was being warned against helping the young girl.

The following is a letter written by Father Alt to Bishop Stangl:[66]

---

[65] Thomas W. Petrisko, Rene Laurentin, Michael J. Fontecchio, *The Fatima Prophecies: At the Doorstep of the World*, St. Andrew's Productions (1998), p. 35-36.

[66] Dr. Goodman, p. 44-47.

Ettleben, September 30, 1974
Most Reverend Bishop:

After much consideration and considerable hesitation, I should now like to acquaint you with a case of spiritual counseling about which I spoke to you very briefly when you were here for a visit.

This is the case of Anneliese Michel of Klingenberg. I will attempt to relate the case to you in order, as it happened.

My friend, Father Roth, came to me one evening and asked me to help him and some of his priest colleagues in solving a case of spiritual counseling. This concerned a girl, Anneliese Michel, whom he had not yet me. According to the opinion of some persons, she was alleged to be possessed or at least molested by the devil. I was supposed to tell, by tuning in on whatever she was radiating, whether she was sick or not.

Suddenly I was able to describe the whole family, father, mother, sisters, and grandmother, something I could not possibly know since I had never seen them. Later all this could be verified. As to Anneliese, I felt an enormous radiation that originated from her neck or, rather, from her thyroid and her head. I did not detect any illness. This, of course, did not permit any conclusions as to whether she was possessed or not.

Two days later a fellow priest (Father Herrmann) visited me who was going to take charge of the case. He handed me two letters, one written by Anna Michel, the other by Anneliese. I was unable to read them because, all of a sudden, I became so nauseated that I thought that at any moment I was going to faint. I experienced a strange excitation such as I had never been subject to before, considerably frightening and startling my fellow priest, who was a witness to all of this. Naturally, even this experience, of course, did not prove we were dealing with a case of possession.

That evening I celebrated Mass. I was mentally prepared for the transubstantiation (the moment when bread and wine becomes the body and blood of Jesus) and also included that unknown girl in the sacrifice. All of a sudden something hit me in the back, the air turned cold and, at the same time, there was an intense stench as though something was burning. I had to lean against the altar. Only with great effort and only a dint of considerable concentration was I able to speak the rest of the text. I felt deeply distressed, as if a negative force were surrounding me, which, however, aside from vexing me, could inflict no real harm.

After the Mass I went to a fellow priest and reported everything to him calmly and in detail.

The subsequent night was the most restless I have ever spent. I had taken a very effective sleeping pill, on that previously had always helped, but I could find no rest. My apartment was filled with a variety of stenches, as though something were burning of dung, of an open sewer, of fecal matter and these kept alternating. It didn't matter whether I reached out to the rosary or whether I spoke some other prayer, the stench continued. It was literally infernal. In addition, there was an occasional loud thumping in my wardrobe. I lay in bed, feeling sorely pressed. I tried to pray. In my own words I spoke an exorcism, thinking of my priestly power. For a few minutes I felt easier, but I was simultaneously ice cold and yet bathed in perspiration. In my extremity, I called to Father Pio for help, since I knew he had experienced similar tribulations. Nothing happened. I repeated my prayer to him and suddenly my room was filled with such an intense fragrance of violets that I thought I had dumped aftershave lotion on my pajamas. But it smelled only of my own sweat. Strangely, at the same time I stopped perspiring and my body felt warm. I breathed with relief and then only to discover, to my amazement, that my field of vision had been very much narrowed, and that my color perception was reduced. Now I was able to see colors once more in their normal intensity. The pressure on my head had disappeared. Before having to get up, I fell into an hour's restful sleep. "My night" had lasted from eleven the previous evening until five o'clock in the morning.

When, the following evening I told my fellow priest about all of this, they were suddenly able to smell the same strange stench. The entire parish house smelled as though of burning, although the windows were open.

The "molestations" did return a few more times, but they became less vivid, and if I prayed the exorcism prayer to myself, they stopped quite abruptly. Occasionally it was as if I had to struggle against them.

In the evening I took a walk with my friend, Father Roth, and once more as we talked about Anneliese Michel, we smelled the same series of stenches. Finally, now, I heard some of the details about the girl's affliction. [He listed them here-omitted] A few weeks later I also met her personally. She was very depressed, but in our conversation she was able to express herself very clearly, and she obviously had a considerable gift of analysis.

During the trial, Father Alt described subsequent walking visions he had experienced. The German government prosecutors were not impressed, and evaluated the priest has having pseudo-hallucinations.

The Last Days Before Exorcism

Before the bishop finally granted permission for the exorcism of Anneliese, one of the last straws occurred on August 1, 1975. Father Alt was visiting Anneliese in Wurzburg. The priest found her in deep despair. They began to pray a rosary together, and Anneliese was unable to continue as tears ran down her face.

As he was leaving, Father Alt prayed the *exorcismus probativus* prayer to himself. Despite taking her medication, Anneliese stood abruptly as if to defend herself. She ripped the rosary to pieces. When her friend Peter arrived, Anneliese told him to leave, speaking in a deep guttural voice. Father Alt was now convinced of Anneliese's possession. Something had changed. His prayers were now providing little to no relief.

Father Alt finally realized the depth of Anneliese's despair when he was leaving. He found a discarded piece of paper with the following notes in Anneliese's handwriting:[67]

> … courage leaves, to say what I wanted.
> I am a sinner; I have clearly recognized that in the chapel today, even if I imagined something different.
> I have no courage, despaired.
> I am afraid that my priest… my
> no trust
> I am standing at the crossroads, either… life or death…
> Grievously injured…
> through the years, I no longer defended
> myself … not now either…
> I became desperate after Holy Communion,
> in spirit and heart. An iron chain is pressing
> around my heart. Fear, terror… my spirit is lame, if it
> becomes free, freer… right away despair rises
> the worst of it is that I have no choice anymore, I see

---

[67] Dr. Goodman, p. 73, 75-76.

that sometimes clear like lightning, hopelessness sits
at the root where life is
it has become a condition
pride, unspeakable pride will not set me free
when I speak, my heart does not speak along
I am afraid that people despair in me paralysis
still I give myself every glimmer of hope… newly up…
fettered
… things will get worse and worse for me
day after day if no
dam will be constructed.

During these last days, Anneliese's friends reported that their group prayer began to physically hurt Anneliese and she stopped attending Holy Mass altogether. Anneliese could not get past the entrance to the church. Her legs became unable to bend. Even at home, Anneliese was forced to drag herself along holding onto the furniture.

Anneliese's friend Anna Lippert describes the girl's face suddenly changing in the middle of their conversation: "…her face contracted into a real Fratze, a hideous, grimacing countenance I cannot describe in detail. Her body became completely stiff."[68]

One Sunday afternoon in July 1975, Anneliese's boyfriend, Peter, took her for a walk in the country. The walking was extremely slow at first given the continued stiffness of her legs. Suddenly, she dropped to her knees and remained unresponsive in a trance-like state for some time. After ten minutes, she leapt up and shouted excitedly, "I can walk, look at me! I'm free, I'm free!"[69] She told Peter she had experienced a vision of the Blessed Virgin Mary.

Two months later at Engelberg Monastery, Anneliese experienced a second apparition of the Blessed Mother. The Virgin Mary is reported to have said the following the Anneliese: "It is

---

[68] Ibid., 72.
[69] Fr. Jose Antonio Fortea, ch.5.

a great suffering for my heart that so many souls are lost! It is necessary to do penance for priests, for the youth, and for your country. Would you like to do penance for these souls so that not so many are lost?"[70]

Anneliese was given three days to consider the Virgin Mary's offer, to accept it or reject it. She relayed this to her parents who were very concerned. They watched as Anneliese spent the next days kneeling before a crucifix. Anna, her mother, told her she could not accept the offer, to which Anneliese replied, "I can, Mom. If I don't, souls may be lost."[71]

It appeared to her parents that Anneliese did accept the offer for the next days were filled with additional apparitions of the Blessed Mother. According to Anneliese, she was completely free of her torments for the next weeks.[72]

These would be the last days of freedom Anneliese experience in her life.

In the days before her exorcisms would begin, Anneliese's behavior grew increasingly more erratic and suggestive of demonic possession. For example, her parents report that Anneliese began to eat flies and spiders; urinate on the kitchen floor; kick, punch, and bite her family; hide under the kitchen table and bark like a dog; and tear holy pictures from the wall and rip them up, along with rosaries and crucifixes.

Later, during a short lucid interval, Anneliese would describe August 15, the Feast of the Assumption of the Blessed Virgin Mary, as the worst day of her life. She was prevented from entering church on this holy day of obligation by an invisible force and, when she recited the prayers of deliverance and exorcism, it felt like she had plunged her hands into a wasps nest. Her hands and feet would later bear the marks of the stigmata.

---

[70] Interview of Fr. Fortea with Father Ernst Alt and Winifried Erb, January 9, 2007.

[71] Ibid.

[72] Interview of Fr. Fortea with Anna Michel, Anneliese's mother, September 2006.

The Exorcisms Begin

After denying the initial requests for the exorcism of Anneliese, Bishop Stangl finally wrote to Father Renz on September 16, 1975 charging him to proceed with the terms of Canon 1151.[73] A bishop's permission is needed to perform an exorcism, because the Church's power over evil is geographically assigned through the dioceses and reposed in the person of the bishop.

The first exorcism began around 4:00pm on September 24, 1975. Though held down by three men, Anneliese continued to struggle and howl like a dog as the priests prayed over here and sprinkled her with holy water. Anneliese kept repeating, "stop with" or "put away that shit" (holy water). Unlike other documented exorcisms, Anneliese was completely aware of what was taking place. When asked what she saw, Anneliese said, "I only observed and had no influence on what was happening. I am only in the background, just looking on."[74]

Together, Fathers Renz and Alt carried out the Rite of Exorcism 67 times over a ten-month period. They held one or two exorcism sessions each week, some of which lasted up to four hours.

Besides the sheer number of times the Rite of Exorcism was performed, Anneliese's awareness of the proceedings, and the special involvement of the Blessed Virgin Mary, there were a number of unique features to Anneliese's exorcisms. Many of the sessions were also recorded. Excerpts from the recordings will be included below.

Another unique feature of the exorcism was Anneliese's repetitive and seemingly obsessive genuflecting. Genuflection is an act of reverence in which a person kneels onto one or both knees. Anneliese would genuflect as many as six hundred times during each exorcism session. Eventually, the ligaments in her knees ruptured.

---

[73] Ibid.
[74] Fr. Jose Antonio Fortea, ch.6.

On June 30, 1976, during what would be her last rite of exorcism before her death, Anneliese was too weak and emaciated to genuflect on her own. Taking her by the arms, Anneliese's parents helped her raise and lower herself to her knees.

Figure 16: Anneliese in her last days

Anneliese, along with Fathers Renz and Alt, were convinced that she had been possessed by several demons and condemned souls, including Lucifer, Judas Iscariot, Nero, Cain, Hitler, and Fleischmann, a disgraced Frankish priest from the 16th century. These frequently spoke through her, conversing regularly with the priests.

While "exorcism" principally refers to the expulsion of demons, it can also refer to the souls of the condemned. This is the case with Judas, of whom Scripture describes as "the son of perdition" (John 17:12). Though we cannot take the words of the liars as fact, it is likely that Judas is joined in hell by Hitler, Nero, and the rest.

Demons Terrorized by the Rosary

After the release of the film *The Exorcism of Emily Rose*, a German website posted audio in which we hear the real Anneliese's voice during one of the exorcisms.

The website claimed to have obtained the audio from one of the 43 taped recordings made during the 67 rites of exorcism that Anneliese endured. The priests can be heard talking about the ghosts of Cain, Nero, and Hitler, who Anneliese believed had taken over her body.

The following is an excerpt from the transcripts:[75]

> Priest: It's the month of the rosary, did you know that?
> Demon: Yes, but (only) the fewest pray.
> Priest: The fewest pray?
> Demon: Yes, and in church, all too few pray because the priests think it's unfashionable.
> Priest: Yes?
> Demon: Yes!
> Priest: All of them?
> Demon: Almost! If only the [expletive] had a clue ...
> Priest: Why do you fear the rosary?
> Demon: Why? Why? Why?
> Priest: Yes, why?
> Demon: Because it ...
> Priest: Because? *Hic me* ... !
> Demon: Because ... Because it is ... No, I will say it not.

---

[75] The statements from these transcripts are confirmed by those found in Father Fortea's book and interviews.

Priest: *Hic me dicere Deus!* (Tell me this by God!)
Demon: Because it is a strong w... shut your mouth! Yes!
Priest: Because it is a strong weapon?
Demon: YES.
Priest: Against Satan...
Demon: Yes, yes!
Priest: ...and all demons?
Demon: Yes, against us. I must say it.
Priest: The rosary is a powerful weapon against ...
Demon: YES!
Priest: ... against Satan and all demons.
Demon: But many do not believe it. They think it's a thing for women, fortunately.
Priest: Who is to blame for that?
Demon: We are!

The demons also diagnosed as errors several other modern developments in the Church. These included the removal of communion rails from around the altar, religious sisters not wearing habits, pressure to allow priests to get married, diminished obedience to the pope, and preaching that the Devil and demons do not exist except metaphorically.

The demons also claimed credit for lies concerning abortion. The demons were compelled to admit the truth: "That abortion ... is murder ... and it doesn't matter which month (the abortion takes place)."

To an outside observer, this may appear as exactly the kind of indictments a conservative Catholic would be expected to make, possessed or not. Nevertheless, it is disturbing that the demons, themselves, are claiming credit for these modern alterations of tradition.

Transcripts of Lucifer and Judas

The following transcript is from one of the first exorcism sessions on September 29, 1975, as recorded in Father Fortea's book on Anneliese.[76] According to Father Renz, Anneliese began to tremble when he arrived for this session.

Lucifer: "The pretentious one is obsessed. This is our work. She cannot take any exams. I'll take care of it. The snotnose is cursed. I will not let her free. I will not get out alone. And we are so many inside her! The snotty slut is ours! You have to pray much more. By order of that one [Virgin Mary] they should still recite… [Rosary] or else, we cannot come out. This affair will last at least for half a year still. By order of that Lady, people should fast. She was cursed from the beginning. She was cursed before birth!"

Judas: "People standing during Holy Communion. This pleases me more than kneeling, I hate it. That thing that you wear, [cassock] the great majority do not wear it any more. They no longer obey the Pope in Rome. It is the one in Rome who keeps the Church going. [To Father Renz] I know you have been to China and there you have offended me much. You snatched souls from me. The one from Frankfurt [Father Rodewyk] has expelled me several times, but now he can no longer do so as he is old. That other one [Gertraud], goes down there to Portugal [Fatima] and preaches of that one [the Virgin Mary] and speaks of the apparitions in 1917. No one believes in them nowadays. That one is taking so many from me, the snotty slut, that stupid, that cursed one."

---

[76] Ibid., ch. 6.

Testing Anneliese

Several tests can be performed on a person to determine if they are truly possessed or merely suffering from a schizophrenic or other psychiatric episode.

While a possessed person drinking holy water is not unheard of, Father Renz brought in three unmarked glasses of water: one contained holy water from Lourdes, one San Damiano water, and the third tap water. When Anneliese picked up the water from San Damiano she commented: "San Damiano shit water."[77] Anneliese drank only the tap water.

Knowledge of foreign or archaic languages unknown to the possessed person is also strong evidence of a true possession. During an exorcism session, Father Renz would typically read from the text of the rite. Once, while Renz was reciting the Latin prayers without the aid of the text, Anneliese corrected his mistakes and admonished him for his poor Latin skills. Anneliese would also immediately respond to questions addressed to her in Chinese or Dutch.

Anneliese also demonstrated unlikely knowledge from the life of Fleischmann, a disgraced Frankish priest from the 16th century, who claimed to be one of her possessors. Fleischmann had been a priest in the Ettleben parish in which Father Alt had served. Alt had come across historical documents describing Fleischmann's offenses, including drunkenness and murder, though he had never shared such with Anneliese. Alt was somewhat shaken by the encounter with Fleischmann as he had also experienced unexplained noises at the Ettleben parish rectory, including doors slamming, footsteps up and down the stairs, and knocking while nobody was present.

---

[77] Ibid., ch. 6.

The End & Our Lady of Fatima

According to the transcripts, Lucifer reportedly said the following: "If the message of the Virgin Mary at Fatima is not given due importance and *Humanae Vitae* respected, a new punishment will come."[78]

Things began to change for Anneliese on the October 13, 1975, the Feast of Our Lady of Fatima, which commemorates the last apparition of the Blessed Virgin Mary in Fatima, Portugal in 1917. In the past, Anneliese merely felt the presence of the Blessed Virgin. From here on, however, the Virgin Mary begins to communicate with her directly.

Anneliese described that, when she received these messages from the Blessed Mother, she did not hear or see anything. Instead, she was made to understand. This mystical phenomenon is called "inner locutions." With regard to the demons, however, she said that they were using her voice and she is only a spectator.

The Virgin Mary instructed Anneliese to record what she is told and to relay this to Father Renz.

Here is an excerpt from Anneliese's diary on October 13, 1975:[79]

> *Mother of God:* "You will often receive inspirations of this kind from me from now on. Things will not always be easy for you. Tell this to Father Arnold. Remember, he is to be your spiritual counselor."

Anneliese's experience of the Virgin Mary was very rich at this time, perhaps fortifying her for what lay ahead. Here is another excerpt from Anneliese's diary, October 16, 1975:

> *Mother of God:* "You are going to complete the work of Barbara Weigand."

---

[78] Ibid.
[79] Dr. Felicitas D. Goodman, *The Exorcism of Anneliese Michel*

Anneliese: I resist; I can't do that, I say: "She should look for somebody else."

Mother of God: "The judgment day is very, very close. Pray as much as you can for your neighborhood, your kin, your friends and benefactors, for priests and laity, for politicians and the people." Mother of God tells me once more that I would become entirely free in October. (She had said this before, a few days ago, but at that time, I thought that the inspiration was not genuine.)

Though separated by many years it is remarkable how the missions of Barbara Weigand and Anneliese intertwined with each other, as well as that of the Blessed Mother. Excerpt from Anneliese's diary, October 17, 1975:

Mother of God: "I want the dissemination of Barbara Weigand's mission."

Figure 17: Anneliese's boyfriend Peter, along with Josef and Anna Michel and Father Arnold Renz attend the funeral

A Matter for the Law

Around Easter, Anneliese's convulsions returned with a greater ferocity, but still no doctor or medical professional was called. She began to refuse food and drink, forcing herself to fast believing that it would rid her of Satan's influence.

On July 1, 1976 Anneliese died of dehydration and malnourishment. She weighed only 68 lbs.

She was buried at the outer edges of a cemetery near to her home. Her resting place is normally an area reserved for illegitimate children and suicides.

After an official investigation into her death, Father Arnold Renz and Pastor Ernst Alt alongside Anneliese's parents, Josef and Anna, were charged with negligent homicide. The court case which took place two years after her death in 1978 become a world-wide sensation.

On March 30, 1978, the trial began in the district court of Aschaffenburg, Germany. The courtroom sitting area was occupied primarily by media persons from Germany and abroad.

At the time, it was the first official and public case of exorcism in Germany in approximately fifty years, and the only known case to have been recorded on audio tapes.

All four defendants were found guilty of negligent homicide and sentenced to six months in prison, suspended with three years' probation.

The government had the contempt to convict Anneliese's family and priests, but not the conviction to imprison them.

An Unofficial Saint

Anneliese wrote in her diary on October 20, 1975 words given to her by Jesus: "You will become a great saint."[80] Her diary records that she wrote these words, which she believed arrogant, only because Jesus had scolded her for *not* recording them.

Anneliese wrote in her diary on October 24, 1975 more words from Jesus: "You will suffer a great deal and do penance, even now. But your sufferings, your sadness and desperation, will help me save souls."[81]

It seems we are still holding vigil for the time when Anneliese's cause for sainthood will advance.

There are several factors which might prove a saint's cause post-mortem, including the working of miracles by the person's intercession, liquefaction of their blood, and their remains remaining free of decay.

In 1978, almost two years after her death, the body of Anneliese Michel was dug up. Her parents' desire to move her from the cheap coffin in which she was buried was allegedly used as an excuse to exhume her body. It's said they were acting on a message received from a nun who had had a vision that Anneliese's body was still intact.

Official reports state that the body showed consistent deterioration. Photos of the exhumed body were never released, and Anneliese's parents were prohibited from witnessing the exhumation. From a distance, they could however see her grave from the bedroom of their home, where her mother still lives today.

Anneliese is far from forgotten, however.

Over 30 years later Anneliese is venerated by small groups of Catholics who honor her as an unofficial saint. Pilgrims from around the world regularly visit her grave, leaving handwritten notes of thanks and gratitude as they sing and pray for

---

[80] Fr. Fortea, ch.6
[81] Ibid.

the young woman they believe sacrificed her own life to atone for the sins of others.

"I know that we did the right thing because I saw the sign of Christ in her hands. She was bearing stigmata and that was a sign from God that we should exorcise the demons. She died to save other lost souls, to atone for their sins."

– Anna Michel (Anneliese's mother, 2005)

Nicola Aubrey, 1565[82]

Introduction:
The Apologetical Exorcism

The exorcism of Nicola Aubrey is remarkable for several reasons: first, for the sheer number of eyewitnesses to the woman's possession;[83] second, for its powerful statement of the Real Presence of Christ in the Eucharist; and, not the least of which, for its unique historical context.

Mademoiselle Aubrey found herself possessed in the thick of the Protestant Revolution,[84] in particular the height of tensions between French Catholics and the Huguenots, the French Calvinists, following the Edict of Amboise.[85] The expulsion of

---

[82] Father Michael Muller, *The Holy Sacrifice of the Mass*, C.Ss.R. (Imprimatur: Archbishop McClosky, New York - 1884), chapter 5.

[83] Irena Dorota Backus, *Guillaume Postel et Jean Boulaese: De Summopere* (1566) *et Le Miracle De Laon* (1566), Droz: 1995.

[84] It is more accurate to described the Protestants' departure from the Catholic Church as a "revolution" than "reformation", as a reformation would have involved the dissidents remaining in the Church, not establishing a myriad of new schismatic churches. For more on this topic, historian Trent Horn has written on the topic.

[85] The Edict of Amboise, also known as the Edict of Pacification, was signed at the Château of Amboise on March 19, 1563 by Catherine de Medici, acting as regent for her son Charles IX of France. The treaty officially ended the first phase of the French Wars of Religion. Moreover, the treaty restored peace to France by guaranteeing the Huguenots religious privileges and freedoms.

Mademoiselle Aubrey's possessors became a competition between Catholics and Calvinists over the legitimacy of their respective churches, at least for the Calvinists.

This was not the only time, nor even the first time, that rival churches attempted to imitate the Church's sovereignty over the powers of evil.

The Book of Acts chronicles the failure of some Jewish scribes to exorcise a powerful demon, despite attempting to do so in the name of Jesus. The Jew's use of the name of Christ was futile, because they themselves had not embraced the Gospel and become members of the Church.

Here is the passage from Acts 19:13-17, regarding the Sons of Sceva:

> Then some of the itinerant Jewish exorcists undertook to pronounce the name of the Lord Jesus over those who had evil spirits, saying, "I adjure you by the Jesus whom Paul preaches." Seven sons of a Jewish high priest named Sceva were doing this. But the evil spirit answered them, "Jesus I know, and Paul I know; but who are you?" And the man in whom the evil spirit was leaped on them, mastered all of them, and overpowered them, so that they fled out of that house naked and wounded. And this became known to all residents of Ephesus, both Jews and Greeks; and fear fell upon them all; and the name of the Lord Jesus was extolled. Many also of those who were now believers came, confessing and divulging their practices. And a number of those who practiced magic arts brought their books together and burned them in the sight of all.

Note, also, in the above passage from Acts, how the name of Jesus wielded by the Church also resulted in the burning of books of magic and witchcraft.

It is not enough simply to confess the Name of Jesus if one hopes to overcome the power of Satan; one has to be incorporated into Christ, that is into the Church, which is His Mystical Body. What's more, an ordained representative of this Church, properly authorized, is the sharpest sword to slay these demons.

The history described in Acts repeated itself in the 1500s when multiple groups left the Church and nevertheless attempted to perform exorcisms.

Such were the circumstances of the case of Nicola Aubrey, a possessed girl in Vervins, Picardy in France. Again, like the other possessions described in this book, this happened to Nicola when she was a young teen. The events narrated below took place on November 8, 1565 and lasted until February 8, 1566 and were witnessed by thousands.

The following account of the exorcism of Nicola Aubrey was written by Father Michael Muller in the 1880s.

Father Muller's Account of the Vervins Exorcism

It is indeed a remarkable fact that, as the devil made use of Luther, an apostate monk, to abolish the Mass and deny the Real Presence; in like manner, God made use of His arch-enemy, the devil, to prove the Real Presence. He repeatedly forced him publicly to profess his firm belief in it, to confound the heretics for their disbelief, and acknowledge himself vanquished by Our Lord in the Blessed Sacrament.

For this purpose, God allowed a certain Mme. Nicola Aubrey, an innocent person, to become possessed by Beelzebub and twenty-nine other evil spirits. The possession took place on the eighth of November, 1565, and lasted until the eighth of February, 1566.

The Exorcist: Father de Motta

Her parents took her to Father de Motta,[86] a pious priest of Vervins, in order that he might expel the demon by exorcisms of the Church. Father de Motta tried several times to expel the evil spirit by applying the sacred relics of the holy cross, but he could not succeed; Satan would not depart.

At last, inspired by the Holy Ghost, he resolved to expel the devil by means of the sacrament of Our Lord's Body and Blood. Whilst Nicola was lying in a state of unnatural lethargy, Father de Motta placed the Blessed Sacrament upon her lips, and instantly the infernal spell was broken; Nicola was restored to consciousness, and received Holy Communion with every mark of devotion.

As soon as Nicola had received the sacred Body of Our Lord, her face became bright and beautiful as the face of an angel, and all who saw her were filled with joy and wonder, and they blessed God from their inmost hearts. With the permission of God, Satan returned and again took possession of Nicola.

Failed Exorcisms by Calvinists

As the strange circumstances of Nicola's possession became known everywhere, several Calvinist preachers came with their followers, to "expose this popish cheat," as they said.

On their entrance, the devil saluted them mockingly, called them by name, and told them that they had come in obedience to him. One of the preachers took his Protestant prayer book,

---

[86] Father Pierre de la Motte was a member of the Dominican order, the religious order founded in France by the Spanish priest Saint Dominic in the 13th century.

and began to read it with a very solemn face.

The devil laughed at him, and putting on a most comical look, he said: "Ho! Ho! My good friend; do you intend to expel me with your prayers and hymns? Do you think that they will cause me any pain? Don't you know that they are mine? I helped to compose them!"

"I will expel thee in the name of God," said the preacher, solemnly.

"You!" said the devil mockingly. "You will not expel me either in the name of God, or in the name of the devil. Did you ever hear of one devil driving out another?"

"I am not a devil," said the preacher, angrily, "I am a servant of Christ."

"A servant of Christ, indeed!" said Satan, with a sneer. "What! I tell you, you are worse than I am. I believe, and you do not want to believe. Do you suppose that you can expel me from the body of this miserable wretch? Ha! Go first and expel all the devils that are in your own heart!"

The preacher took his leave, somewhat discomfited. On going away, he said, turning up the whites of his eyes, "O Lord, I pray thee, assist this poor creature!"

"And I pray Lucifer," cried the evil spirit, "that he may never leave you, but may always keep you firmly in his power, as he does now. Go about your business, now. You are all mine, and I am your master."

On the arrival of the priest, several of the Protestants went away – they had seen and heard more than they wanted. Others, however, remained; and great was their terror when they saw how the devil writhed and howled in agony, as soon as the Blessed Sacrament was brought near him. At last the evil spirit departed, leaving Nicola in a state of unnatural trance.

While she was in this state, several of the preachers tried to open her eyes, but they found it impossible to do so. The priest then placed the Blessed Sacrament on Nicola's lips, and instantly she was restored to consciousness. Rev. Father de Motta then turned to the astonished preachers, and said: "Go now, ye preachers of the new Gospel; go and relate everywhere what you have seen and heard. Do not deny any longer that Our Lord Jesus Christ is really and truly present in the Blessed Sacrament of the altar. Go now, and let not human respect hinder you from confessing the truth."

During the exorcisms of the following days, the devil was forced to confess that he was not to be expelled at Vervins, and that he had with him twenty-nine devils, among whom were three powerful demons: Cerberus, Astaroth, and Legio. On the third of January, 1566, the bishop arrived at Vervins, and began the exorcism in the church, in the presence of an immense multitude.

"I command thee, in the name and by power of the real presence of Our Lord in the Blessed Sacrament, to depart instantly," said the bishop to Satan in a solemn voice.

Satan was, at last, expelled the second time by means of the Blessed Sacrament. On leaving, he paralyzed the left arm and right foot of Nicola, and also made her left arm longer than her right; and no power on earth could cure this strange infirmity, until some weeks after, when the devil was at last completely and irrevocably expelled. Nicola was now taken to the celebrated pilgrimage of Our Lady at Liesse, especially since the devil seemed to fear that place so much. Next day Father de Motta began the exorcism in the church of Our Lady at Liesse, in the presence of an immense multitude. He took the Blessed Sacrament in his hand, and, showing it to the demon, he said: "I command thee, in the name of the living God, the great Emmanuel Whom thou seest here present, and in Whom thou believest."

"Ah, yes!" shrieked the demon, "I believe in Him." And the devil howled again as he made this confession, for it was wrung from him by the power of Almighty God.

"I command thee, then, in His Name," said the priest, "to quit this body instantly."

At these words, and especially at the sight of the Blessed Sacrament, the devil suffered the most frightful torture. At one moment the body of Nicola was rolled up like a ball; then again she became fearfully swollen. At one time her face was unnaturally lengthened, then excessively widened, and sometimes it was as red as scarlet. Her eyes, at times, protruded horribly, and then again sunk deeply into her skull. Her tongue hung down to her chin; it was sometimes black, sometimes red, and sometimes spotted like a toad. The priest still continued to urge and torture Satan. "Accursed spirit!" he cried, "I command thee, in the Name and by the real presence of Our Lord Jesus Christ here in the Blessed Sacrament, to depart instantly from the body of this poor creature."

"Ah, yes!" cried Satan, howling wildly, "twenty-six of my companions shall leave this instant, for they are forced to do so."

The people in the church now began to pray with great fervor. Suddenly Nicola's limbs began to crack, as if every bone in her body were breaking; a pestilential vapor came forth from her mouth, and twenty-six devils departed from her, never more to return. Nicola then fell into an unnatural swoon, from which she was aroused only by the Blessed Sacrament. On recovering her senses, and receiving Holy Communion, Nicola's face shone like the face of an angel. The priest still continued to urge the demon, and used every means to expel him.

"I will not leave, unless commanded by the bishop of Leon," answered the demon, angrily.

Nicola was now taken to Pierrepont, where one of the demons, name Legio, was expelled by means of the Blessed Sacrament. Next morning Nicola was brought to the church. Scarcely had she quitted the house, when the devil again took possession of her. The bishop who was requested to exorcise Nicola, prepared himself for this terrible task by prayer and fasting, and other works of penance. On arrival of Nicola in the Church, the exorcism began. "How many are you in this body?" asked the bishop.

"There are three of us," answered the evil spirit.

"What are your names?"

"Beelzebub, Cerberus, and Astaroth."

"What has become of the others?" asked the bishop.

"They have been expelled," answered Satan.

"Who expelled them?"

"Ha!" cried the devil, gnashing his teeth, "it was He whom you hold in your hand, there on the paten." The devil meant our dear Lord in the Blessed Sacrament.

The bishop then held the Blessed Sacrament near the face of Nicola. The demon writhed and howled in agony. "Ah, yes! I will go, I will go!" he shrieked, "but I shall return."

Suddenly Nicola became stiff and motionless as marble. The bishop then touched her lips with the Blessed Sacrament, and in an instant she was fully restored to consciousness. She received Holy Communion, and her countenance now shone with a wondrous, supernatural beauty. Next day Nicola was brought again to the Church, and the exorcism began as usual. The bishop took the Blessed Sacrament in his hand, held it near the face of Nicola, and said:

"I command thee in the name of the living God, and by the real presence of Our Lord Jesus Christ here in the sacrament of the altar, to depart instantly from the body of this creature of God, and never more to return."

"No! No!" shrieked the devil, "I will not go. My hour is not yet come."

"I command thee to depart. Go forth, impure, accursed spirit! Go forth!" and the bishop held the Blessed Sacrament close to Nicola's face.

"Stop! stop!", shrieked Satan; "let me go! I will depart – but I shall return." And instantly Nicola fell into the most frightful convulsions. A black smoke was seen issuing from her mouth, and she fell again into a swoon.

The Second Round of Exorcisms

During her stay in Leon, Nicola was carefully examined by Catholic and Protestant physicians. Her left arm, which had been paralyzed by the devil, was found entirely without feeling. The doctors cut into the arm with a sharp knife; they burnt it with fire; they drove pins and needles under the nails of the fingers; but Nicola felt not pain; her arm was utterly insensible. Once, while Nicola was lying in a state of unnatural lethargy, the doctors gave her some bread soaked in wine (it was what the Protestants call their communion, or Lord's Supper); they rubbed her limbs briskly; they threw water in her face; they pierced her tongue until the blood flowed; they tried every possible means to arouse her, but in vain! Nicola remained cold and motionless as marble. At last, the priest touched the lips of Nicola with the Blessed Sacrament, and instantly she was restored to consciousness, and began to praise God.

The miracle was so clear, so palpable, that one of the doctors, who was a bigoted Calvinist, immediately renounced his errors, and became a Catholic. Several times, also, the Protestants touched Nicola's face with a host which was not consecrated, and which, consequently, was only bread, but Satan was not the least tormented by this. He only ridiculed their efforts.

On the twenty-seventh of January, the bishop, after having walked in solemn procession with the clergy and the faithful, began the exorcism in church, in the presence of a vast multitude of Protestants and Catholics. The bishop now held the Blessed Sacrament close to the face of Nicola. Suddenly a wild, unearthly yell rings through the air -- a black, heavy smoke issues from the mouth of Nicola. The demon Astaroth is expelled forever. During the exorcism which took place on the first of February, the bishop said:

"O accursed spirit! Since neither prayer, nor the holy gospels, neither the exorcisms of the Church, nor the holy relics, can compel thee to depart, I will now show thee thy Lord and Master, and by His power I command thee."

During the exorcism, which took place after Mass, the bishop held the Blessed Sacrament in his hand, and said: "O accursed spirit, arch-enemy of the ever-blessed God! I command thee, by the precious blood of Jesus Christ here present, to depart from this poor woman! Depart accursed, into the everlasting flames of hell!"

At these words, and especially at the sight of the Blessed Sacrament, the demon was so fearfully tormented, and the appearance of Nicola was so hideous and revolting, that the people turned away their eyes in horror. At last a heavy sigh was heard, and a cloud of black smoke issued from the mouth of Nicola. Cerberus was expelled. Again Nicola fell into a death-like swoon, and again she was brought to consciousness only by means of the Blessed Sacrament. During the exorcism which took place on the seventh day of February, the bishop said to Satan:

"Tell me. Why hast thou taken possession of this honest and virtuous Catholic woman?"

"I have done so by permission of God. I have taken possession of her on account of the sins of the people. I have done it to show my Calvinists that there are devils who can take possession of man whenever God permits it. I know they do not want to believe this, but I will show them that I am the devil. I have taken possession of this creature in order to convert them, or to harden them in their sins; and, by the Sacred Blood, I will perform my task."

This answer filled all who heard it with horror. "Yes," answered the bishop, solemnly, "God desires to unite all men in the only holy faith. As there is but one God, so there can be but one true religion. A religion like that which the Protestants have invented, is but a hollow mockery. It must fall. The religion established by Our Lord Jesus Christ is the only true one; it alone shall last forever. It is destined to unite all men within its sacred embrace, so that there shall be but one sheepfold and one shepherd. This divine Shepherd is Our Lord Jesus Christ, the invisible head of the holy Roman Catholic Church, whose visible head is our holy Father the Pope, successor of St. Peter."

The devil was silent – he was put to shame before the entire multitude. He was expelled once more by means of the Blessed Sacrament. In the afternoon of the same day the devil began to cry: "Ah! Ha! You think that you can expel me in this way. You have not the proper attendance of a bishop. Where are the dean and the archdean? Where are the royal judges? Where is the chief magistrate, who was frightened out of his wits that night, in the prison? Where is the procurator of the king? Where are his attorneys and counselors? Where is the clerk of the court?" (The devil mentioned each of these by name.) "I will not depart until all are assembled. Were I to depart now, what proof could you give to the king of all that has happened? Do you think that people will believe you so easily? No! No! There are many who would make objections. The testimony of these common country-people here will have but little weight. It is a torment to me that I must tell you what you have to do. I am forced to do it. Ha! Cursed be the hour in which I first took possession of this vile wretch.

"I find little pleasure in thy prating," answered the bishop. "There are witnesses enough here. Those whom you have mentioned are not necessary. Depart! then; give glory to God. Depart – go to the flames of hell!"

"Yes, I shall depart, but not today. I know full well that I must depart. My sentence is passed; I am compelled to leave."

"I care not for thy jabbering," said the bishop, "I shall expel thee by the power of God: by the Precious Blood of Our Lord Jesus Christ."

"Yes, I must yield to you," shrieked the demon wildly. "It tortures me that I must give you this honor."

The bishop now took the Blessed Sacrament in his hand, and held it close to the face of the possessed woman. At last, Satan was compelled to flee once more. The next morning, after the procession was ended, the Holy Sacrifice of the Mass was offered up as usual. During the consecration, the possessed woman was twice raised over six feet into the air, and then fell back heavily upon the platform. As the bishop, just before the Pater Noster, took the Sacred Host once more in his hand, and raised it with the chalice, the possessed woman was again whisked into the air, carrying with her the keepers, fifteen in number, at least six feet above the platform; and, after a while, she fell heavily back on the ground.

At this sight, all present were filled with amazement and terror. A German Protestant named Voske fell on his knees; he burst into tears; he was converted. "Ah!" cried he, "I now believe firmly that the devil really possesses this poor creature. I believe that it is really the body and blood of Jesus Christ which expels him. I believe firmly. I will no longer remain a Protestant." After Mass, the exorcism began as usual.

The Real Presence of Jesus in the Eucharist

"Now, at last," said the bishop, "thou must depart. Away with thee, evil spirit!"

"Yes," said Satan, "it is true that I must depart, but not yet. I will not go before the hour is come in which I first took possession of this wretched creature."

At last the bishop took the Sacred Host in his hand, and said: "In the name of the adorable Trinity: Father, Son, and Holy Ghost – in the name of the sacred body of Jesus Christ here present – I command thee, wicked spirit, to depart."

"Yes, yes, it is true!" shrieked the demon wildly; "It is true. It is the body of God. I must confess it, for I am forced to do so. Ha! It tortures me that I must confess this, but I must. I speak the truth only when I am forced to do it. The truth is not from me. It comes from my Lord and Master. I have entered this body by the permission of God."

The bishop now held the Blessed Sacrament close to the face of the possessed woman. The demon writhed in fearful agony. He tried in every way to escape from the presence of Our Lord in the Blessed Sacrament. At length a black smoke was seen issuing from the mouth of Nicola. She fell into a swoon, and was restored to consciousness only by means of the Blessed Sacrament. The eighth of February, the day appointed by God on which Satan was to leave Nicola forever, arrived at last. After the solemn procession, the bishop began the last exorcism.

"I shall not ask thee any longer," said the bishop to Satan, "when thou intendest to leave, I will expel thee instantly by the power of the living God, and by the precious Body and Blood of Jesus Christ, His beloved Son, here present in the Sacrament of the Altar."

"Ha, yes!" shrieked the demon. "I confess that the Son of God is here really and truly present. He is my Lord and Master. It tortures me to confess it, but I am forced to do so." Then he repeated several times, with a wild, unearthly howl: "Yes, it is true. I must confess it. I am forced to leave, by the power of God's body here present. I must – I must depart. It torments me that I must go so soon, and that I must confess this truth. But this truth is not from me; it comes from my Lord and Master, who has sent me hither, and who commands and compels me to confess the truth publicly."

The bishop then took the Blessed Sacrament in his hand, and, holding it on high, he said, with a solemn voice: "O thou wicked, unclean spirit, Beelzebub! Thou arch-enemy of the eternal God! Behold, here present, the precious Body and Blood of Our Lord Jesus Christ, thy Lord and Master! I adjure thee, in the name and by the power of Our Lord and Savior Jesus Christ, true God and true man, who is here present; I command thee to depart instantly and forever from this creature of God. Depart to the deepest depth of hell, there to be tormented forever. Go forth, unclean spirit, go forth – behold here thy Lord and Master!"

At these solemn words, and at the sight of our sacramental Lord, the poor possessed woman writhed fearfully. Her limbs cracked as if every bone in her body were breaking. The fifteen strong men who held her, could scarcely keep her back. They staggered from side to side; they were covered with perspiration. Satan tried to escape from the presence of Our Lord in the Blessed Sacrament. The mouth of Nicola was wide open, her tongue hung down below her chin, her face was shockingly swollen and distorted. Her color changed from yellow to green, and became even gray and blue, so that she no longer looked like a human being; it was rather the face of a hideous, incarnate demon. All present trembled with terror, especially when they heard the wild cry of the demon, which sounded like the loud roar of a wild bull. They fell on their knees, and with tears in their eyes, began to cry out: "Jesus, have mercy!"

Satan is Expelled

The bishop continued to urge Satan. At last the evil spirit departed, and Nicola fell back senseless into the arms of her keepers. She still, however, remained shockingly distorted. In this state she was shown to the judges, and to all the people present; she was rolled up like a ball. The bishop now fell on his knees, in order to give her the Blessed Sacrament as usual. But see! Suddenly the demon returns, wild with rage, endeavors to seize the hand of the bishop, and even tries to grasp the Blessed Sacrament itself. The bishop starts back; Nicola is carried into the air and the bishop rises from his knees, trembling with terror and pale as death.

The good bishop takes courage again; he pursues the demon, holding the Blessed Sacrament in his hand, till at length the demon, overcome by the power of Our Lord's sacred body, goes forth amidst smoke, and lightning, and thunder. Thus was the demon at length expelled forever, on Friday afternoon, at three o'clock, the same day and hour on which Our Lord triumphed over hell by His ever-blessed death.

Nicola was now completely cured; she could move her left arm with the greatest ease. She fell on her knees and thanked God, as well as the good bishop, for all he had done for her. The people wept for joy, and sang hymns of praise and thanksgiving in honor of our dear Lord in the Blessed Sacrament. On all sides were heard the exclamations: "Oh, what a great miracle! Oh, thank God that I witnessed it! Who is there now that can doubt of the real presence of Our Lord Jesus Christ in the Sacrament of the Altar!" Many a Protestant also said: "I believe now in the presence of Our Lord in the Blessed Sacrament; I have seen with my eyes! I will remain a Calvinist no longer. Accursed be those who have hitherto kept me in error! Oh, now I can understand what a good thing is the Holy Sacrifice of the Mass!"

A solemn *Te Deum* was intoned; the organ pealed forth and the bells rung forth a merry chime. The whole city was filled with joy.

This great triumph of Jesus Christ in the Blessed Sacrament over Satan occurred in the presence of more than 150,000 people, in the presence of the ecclesiastical and civil authorities of the city, of Protestants and Catholics alike.[87]

---

[87] Father Muller adds the following: "I have published a lengthy account of this extraordinary affair in a little volume entitled "Triumph of the Blessed Sacrament." These facts are well authenticated by the accounts published in various languages, including French, Italian, Spanish, and German, as I have shown on pages 13, 14, and 15 of the above-mentioned little volume."

Appendix I:
The Roman Ritual of Exorcism, Chapter One, "Instructions for Exorcising Those Possessed by Evil Spirit"

1: The priest who with the particular and explicit permission of his Bishop is about to exorcise those tormented by Evil Spirit, must have the necessary piety, prudence, and personal integrity. He should perform this most heroic work humbly and courageously, not relying on his own strength, but on the power of God; and he must have no greed for material benefit. Besides, he should be of mature age and be respected as a virtuous person.

2: To perform his task correctly, he should be acquainted with the many practical writings of approved authors on the subject of Exorcism. These are omitted here for the sake of brevity. He should, in addition, carefully observe the following few rules which are of major importance.

3: Above all, he must not easily believe that someone is possessed by Evil Spirit. He must be thoroughly acquainted with those signs by which he can distinguish the possessed person from those who suffer from a physical illness. The signs of possession by Evil Spirit are of a peculiar genre. Among others; when the subject speaks unknown languages with many words or understands unknown languages; when he clearly knows about things that are distant or hidden; when he shows a physical strength far above his age or normal condition. These manifestations together with others of the same kind are major indications.

4: To be all the surer, the exorcist should interrogate the subject after one or two exorcism addresses, asking him what he feels in his spirit or in his body. In this way, also, he will find out what words disturb Evil Spirit more than others; and thus he can repeat such words and have greater effect on Evil Spirit.

5: Let the exorcist note for himself the tricks and deceits which Evil Spirits use in order to lead him astray, for they are accustomed to answering falsely. They manifest themselves only under pressure--in the hope that the exorcist will get tired and desist from pressuring them. Or they make it appear that the subject of Exorcism is not possessed at all.

6: Sometimes, Evil Spirit betrays its presence, and then goes into hiding. It appears to have left the body of the possessed free from all molestation, so that the possessed thinks he is completely rid of it. But the exorcist should not, for all that desist until he sees the signs of liberation.

7: Sometimes, also, Evil Spirit throws up every possible obstacle in order to stop the possessed from submitting to Exorcism. Or it tries to persuade him that his affliction is quite natural. Sometimes, during Exorcism, it gets the possessed to go to sleep; or it shows him some vision. But it hides itself, so that the possessed appears to be freed from it.

8: Some Evil Spirits reveal an occult spell and by whom it was made, and the way in which it can be loosened. But the exorcist must beware of having recourse in such matters to witches or warlocks or sorcerers or to any others beyond Church ministers. And let him not rely on any superstitious practice or any other illicit method.

9: Sometimes, Evil Spirit leaves the possessed in peace and even allows him to receive Holy Communion, so that It seems to have gone away. In sum, innumerable are the stratagems and deceits of which the Evil Spirit uses in order to deceive men. The exorcist must practice caution in order not to be deceived by any of them.

10: He must remember, therefore, that Our Lord said there is a species of Evil Spirit which cannot be expelled except by prayer and fasting. Let Him make sure that he and others follow the example of the Holy Fathers and make use of these two principal means of obtaining divine help and of repelling Evil Spirit.

11: If it is convenient, the possessed can be exorcised in a church or in some other religious and appropriate place apart from the public eye. If the subject is ill, or if there is any other good reason, he can be exorcised in a private home.

12: The possessed must be encouraged to pray to God, to fast, and to get spiritual strength from the Sacraments of Confessions and Holy Communion, if he enjoys mental and physical health.

13: The possessed should hold a Crucifix in his hands or have it in front of him. Whenever available, the relics of the saints can be placed on his chest, or on his head. They should be appropriately and safely covered. But let care be taken that these holy things are not treated irreverently and damaged by Evil Spirit. The Holy Eucharist should not be placed on the head or anywhere on the body of the possessed. There is a danger that it will be treated irreverently.

14: The exorcist must not make great speeches or put superfluous questions out of vain curiosity, especially about future events and hidden matters which have nothing to do with his work. He should command the unclean spirit to keep silent and only to respond to what is asked of it. And he must give no credence to Evil Spirit, if it claims to be the soul of some saint or of a dead person or to be the Good Angel.

15: Questions he must ask the possessing Evil Spirit are, for example, the number and name of possessing spirits; when they entered the possessed,; why they entered him; and other questions of the same kind. Let the exorcist restrain the other vanities, mockeries, and foolishnesses of Evil Spirit. He should treat them with contempt. And he should admonish those who are present--who should be few in number--not to take any notice of what Evil Spirit says and not to put any questions to the possessed, Let them pray humbly and fervently to God for the deliverance of the possessed.

16: The exorcist should perform and read the exorcism with command, authority, great faith, humility, and fervor. And, when he sees that the possessing spirit is being tortured mightily, he should multiply all these efforts at pressuring it. Whenever he sees some part of the possessed person's body moving or pierced or some swelling appearing, let him make the Sign of the Cross and sprinkle Holy Water.

17: Let him pay attention also to the words and expressions which disturb Evil Spirit most, and repeat them very often. And when he arrives at the point of Expulsion, let him pronounce that Expulsion again and again, always increasing the punishment. And, if he sees that he is succeeding, let him persevere until he is finally victorious.

18; Finally, let the exorcist beware not to offer any medicine to the possessed or suggest any to him. All this he should leave to the medical doctors.

19: If he is exorcising a woman, he should have with him some reputable women who will hold the possessed when she is tormented and shaken by Evil Spirit. Such women should be of great patience and belong to the family of the possessed. The exorcist must be mindful of scandal and avoid doing or saying anything which could provoke ill for himself or for others.

20: During Exorcism, the exorcist should use the words of the Bible rather than his own or somebody else's. Also, he should command Evil Spirit to state whether it is kept within the possessed because of some magical spell or sorcerer's symbol or some occult documents. For the exorcism to succeed, the possessed must surrender them. If he has swallowed something like that, he will vomit it up. If it is outside his body in some place or other, Evil Spirit must tell the exorcist where it is. When the exorcist finds it, he must burn it.

21: It the possessed person is freed from Evil Spirit, he should be advised to be diligent in avoiding sinful actions and thoughts. If he does not, he could give Evil Spirit a fresh occasion for returning and possessing him. In that case, he would be in a much worse condition than before.

Appendix II:
"Begone Satan!"
by Father Carl Vogl

Begone Satan!
- A Soul-Stirring Account Of Diabolical Possession In Iowa
- After 23 Days' Battle in September, 1928, Devil Was Forced to Leave

Imprimatur
+ JOS. P. BUSCH
Bishop of St Cloud
St. Cloud, July 28, 1935.

Nihil Obstat
RT. REV. JOHN P. DURHAM
Published with permission of Rt. Rev. Alcuin Deutsch, O.S.B., St. John's Abbey
Leaflets with the Exorcism against Satan and the Rebellious Angels published by order of His Holiness, Pope Leo XIII may be had at one cent a copy.

BEGONE SATAN!

A Soul-Stirring Account of Diabolical Possession

Woman Cursed by Her Own Father, Possessed from 14th Year till 40th Year: Devils Appearing: Beelzebub, Lucifer, Judas, Jacob, and Mina

By Father Carl Vogl,
A Witness to These Events

Published by
Rev. Celestine Kapsner, 0. S. B.
St. John's Abbey
Collegeville, Minn.

Foreward

In regard to *Begone Satan*, some persons have asked the question: "Why publish a story of this kind in our age and civilization?" One could answer this by replying that our age and civilization needs to learn anew a lesson that was vainly laughed to scorn in past generations.

During His sojourn here on earth Christ cast out devils at various times. The powers of Christ were transmitted to the Apostles and their successors; and the Church's ordinary rite of ordination to the Priesthood includes the order of exorcist, in which Christ's power to cast out devils is transmitted. The Church, moreover, has a special rite for such exorcisms, and throughout the ages she has witnessed the effective use of it. Her long experience also explains her extreme caution, her extensive investigation of a case, before permitting any exorcism.

For a time it was fashionable to scoff at demoniacal possession as part and parcel of an outmoded superstition of bygone ages of ignorance — like the attitude of a lifetime ago in regard to the miracles of Lourdes. But facts are stubborn, also against the scoffings of so-called enlightened criticism. Stubborn facts cannot be denied even when they baffle all natural explanation. The absurd thing about such a position is that the critics "just know" that supernatural or preternatural phenomena simply "cannot be."

We have become much more sober in our day. And it is a healthy sign that the man of education no longer scoffs so readily at that which he cannot explain. So much has been gained for perennial common sense.

To a great extent the essential matters of Christian faith are beyond the field of natural knowledge. However, any viewpoint that is flatly contradicted by true natural knowledge cannot be a matter of Christian faith. In regard to sin and the Kingdom of Satan, Christian faith teaches Christ's conquest of Satan and Satan's dominion by His death and resurrection. Now this conquest is shared by individual souls in the sacrament of Baptism, the rite of which contains several solemn exorcisms as well as renunciation of Satan and his pomps. In the light of this Christian faith it is not at all surprising that Satan should be regaining something of his hold on men in our day.

For we have in several past centuries witnessed the increased abandonment by men of the Church of Christ, and among non-Catholic denominations the increased abandonment of the sacrament of Baptism. What is this but a great surrender to the powers of evil?

For a succinct statement of the Catholic position on possession by the devil, the reader is referred to the *Catholic Encyclopedia*, article "Possession, Demoniacal."

Virgil Michel, 0. S. B., Ph. D.

Written in German by
REV. CARL VOGL
Translated by
REV. CELESTINE KAPSNER, O.S.B.

Begone Satan!

*A Sensational Expulsion of the Devil
which occurred in Iowa in 1928.*

Nineteen hundred years ago, Christ, the Son of God, came upon this earth. He gained the victory over Satan, the Prince of this World, and founded His own Kingdom, the Church. He vested His Church with the same powers that He had received from the Father. "As the Father sent Me, so I send you."

When preparing her candidates for the ministry, Holy Mother Church hands these powers over to them that they may continue the mission of Christ's Kingdom on earth. Preparatory to Holy Priesthood the candidate receives the so-called minor and major orders. Among the minor orders is one called the Order of Exorcist. When the Bishop confers this order he pronounces the following significant words: You receive also the power to place your hands upon those possessed and through the imposition of the hands, the grace of the Holy Ghost and the words of exorcism you shall drive evil spirits out of the bodies of those so possessed.

The solemn and powerful meaning attached to this ceremony, not conferred in any of the other orders, can be gleaned from the words: Receive and impress upon your mind that you receive the right to place your hands upon those possessed.

Later on the Bishop invites the faithful to join him in asking that he who is to receive this order may be an effective agent in expelling the evil spirit from those possessed. He continues to pray that the candidate may become an approved physician of the Church through the gift of healing conferred upon her by the Almighty Himself.

The Church bases her action on the example of Christ Himself, Who frequently drove out evil spirits and endowed His disciples with full authority to do likewise. The superficial faith of our age regards such an order as superfluous. The reality of hell, devils, and cases of possession have been denied as myths of the dark ages. Even if Christ and the Apostles repeatedly emphasized the powers of the evil spirit, these are looked upon as purely superstitious, That Satan has succeeded in making man so indifferent regarding his actions of misleading men is one of the greatest and most advantageous accomplishments. People rarely listen to anything of a supernatural nature.

Actual happenings of the supernatural in our times are all the more striking therefore and cannot so readily be dismissed by a mere shrug of the shoulders — facts such as the numerous and indisputable miracles at Lourdes, the extraordinary visions, stigmata, abstention from food, and gift of languages of Theresa Neumann, the life of the Cure of Ars who was recently proclaimed a saint of the Church, to whom for 35 years the sight of hell was constantly and really an ordinary experience. No less worthy of note are the facts in the cases of possession occurring in our times: the case of a possessed boy in Wemding, Suabia, Bavaria, 1891 ; the case in St. Michael's Mission in Africa in 1906 of two girls being possessed, one of whom is still living; the noted case of the Chinese woman Lautien in Honan, China, in 1926 and 1929, which was under the direction of Father Peter Heier, S. V. D., of Hague, N. D., now a Missioner in China.

The priest has frequent opportunities for using his power of exorcism. The blessings of holy water, its various uses in the blessing of houses and in the many other blessings and benedictions of the church in her sacramentals, are dependent upon this power. Pope Leo XIII in our own time has composed a powerful and solemn prayer of exorcism for priests against the fallen angels and evil spirits. It is said that this Pope, after God permitted him to see in a vision the great devastation Satan is carrying on in our times, composed the prayer of exorcism in honor of St. Michael that is now recited in the vernacular as one of the prayers after Mass.

Recent Case of Possession and Expulsion in Earling, Iowa

The following soul-stirring case of actual possession and successful expulsion, through the powers given to the Church over the evil one, is all the more striking in view of the above explanations. The facts herein narrated are testified to by the Rev. Joseph Steiger, who was a personal witness of the scenes herein narrated. While conducting a mission in the parish of Earling in 1928, Father Theophilus Riesinger, O. M. Cap., asked the Rev. Pastor for permission to have a certain person, whom he believed possessed by the devil, brought into his parish, and to be permitted to use the solemn formula of exorcism over her while she would be detained in the Convent of the Franciscan Sisters who were active in the .parish. Father Steiger happened to be a personal friend of Father Theophilus for many years past.

"What, another case of possession?" replied the pastor. "Are these cases still on the increase? You have already dispossessed the devil in a number of such cases!"

"That is indeed true. However, the Bishop has again entrusted this case into my hands. The lady in question lives at some distance from Earling. I should like to have her brought here, since it would create too much excitement in her home and perhaps would be the cause of many disturbances to the person herself."

"But why just here in my own parish?"

"It is just here in an outlying country district that the case may be disposed of in a quiet manner. Two places are available, either in the Sisters' Convent or here in the sacristy. So it is quite possible to relieve the unfortunate person of her burden without anybody out in the world becoming aware of it."

"My dear Father, do you really think that the Mother Superior would permit anything like that to take place under her convent roof? I don't believe it. And it would be altogether out of the question to bring the person into my own house."

"My dear friend," smilingly replied the Father, "tell me this one thing. Will you give me your approval, should the Mother Superior be willing?"

"Well, all right, but only under this condition. I do not believe that you will have any success at the convent."

"Thanks for your permission. The case is therefore settled, as the Mother Superior did give her consent from the very beginning. I had already made all arrangements with her for this case provided you would give your full approval."

Thus it was agreed to have the exorcism performed at the convent. The place was situated in the country, and as it was summer time, the people were actively occupied with their work in the open fields.

No one would be any the wiser. Much less would anyone bother himself about what was going on. For safety's sake the case was again submitted to the Bishop, who called the pastor to himself to acquaint him with matters that he might expect to happen.

"So, my Father, you have given your consent to allow this to take place in your parish. Have you thought the matter over sufficiently?"

"Your Lordship, to be honest, I must confess that I was not very anxious to have it. I have a rather strong aversion for such unusual affairs. But Father Theophilus explained that my country parish together with the easy access to the convent would be just suitable for such an undertaking, and so I disliked to refuse."

"As Bishop I will caution you most emphatically that there may be some very serious consequences resulting to you in person. Should the Reverend Father not have enlightened you regarding the matter, then I wish to give you information based upon sound facts and similar experiences. The devil will certainly try his utmost to seek revenge on you, should you be willing that this unfortunate woman be relieved of this terrible oppression."

"Well, I hardly think that it will be as bad as all that. God's protecting hand will not fail me. The devil has no more influence than God permits. And if God will not permit it, the devil will not be able to harm me in the least. So I have no misgivings. I shall keep my word. I have given my consent, and for that very reason I would not care to withdraw it again. And should it entail some sacrifices, I shall be only too glad to bear them if only an immortal soul shall benefit by it and shall be freed from the terrible stranglehold of that infernal being."

The pastor had little suspicion of what the future had in store for him. Today he would hesitate more than once before consenting again so readily. Far be it from him that he should ever live through such experiences again.

The Lady in Question

The unfortunate woman was unknown to the pastor. She lived far from Earling, and up to then he had heard nothing about her. The Capuchin Father had explained to him what her actual condition was, that she was a very pious and respectable person now in her fortieth year. Throughout her youth she led a religious, fervent and blameless life. In fact she approached the sacraments frequently. After her fourteenth year some unusual experiences manifested themselves. She wanted to pray, wanted to go to church and as usual receive Holy Communion. But some interior hidden power was interfering with her plans. The situation became worse instead of improving. Words cannot express what she had to suffer.

She was actually barred from the consolations of the Church, torn away from them by force. She could not help herself in any way and seemed to be in the clutches of some mysterious power. She was conscious of some sinister inner voices that kept on suggesting most disagreeable things to her. These voices tried their utmost to arouse thoughts of the most shameful type within her, and tried to induce her to do things unmentionable and even to bring her to despair. The poor creature was helpless and secretly was of the opinion that she would become insane. There were times when she felt impelled to shatter her holy water font, when she could have attacked her spiritual adviser and could have suffocated him. Yes, there were thoughts urging her to tear down the very house of God.

"Hallucination, a pure hysterical case, nervous spells." Such easy explanations one will hear to account for the experiences. True, similar happenings do occur in nervous and hysterical cases. However, many doctors had this case in charge for years, and the woman was finally examined by the best specialists in the profession. But their thorough examinations resulted in the unanimous conclusion that the woman in question does not betray the least sign of nervousness, that she is normal in the fullest sense. There was not the slightest indication suggesting physical illness. Her undeniable and unusual experiences could not be accounted for. As the doctors could not help her, it was thought to seek results in another field.

Many years passed. Since the natural means, medical aid and professional knowledge, were of no avail, recourse was had to the Church and the supernatural powers of the priesthood. But a reserved and skeptical attitude was maintained for some years towards proceeding with exorcism. Examinations and observations were constantly made. However, it gradually became evident that strange preternatural powers were at play. The woman understood languages which she had never heard nor read. When the priest spoke the language of the Church and blessed her in the Latin tongue, she sensed and understood it at once, and at the same time foamed at the mouth and became enraged about it. When he continued in classical Latin, she regained her former ease. She was conscious at once when some one gave her articles sprinkled with holy water or presented her with things secretly blessed, whereas ordinary secular objects would leave her perfectly indifferent.

In short, when after years of trial and observation she reached her fortieth year, the ecclesiastical authorities were finally convinced that here was a clear case of demoniacal possession. The Church must step in and deliver the poor creature from the powers of the evil one. The cause of the possession could not be ascertained. The woman herself could not give any information about this matter. Only later during the process of solemn exorcism was the cause made known.

Father Theophilus had spent many years giving missions in the United States and was familiar with cases of possession. Since he had already dispossessed the evil one in many instances, Holy Mother Church entrusted this case to him. His stainless career, as well as his successful encounter in numerous possessions, singled him out as the one best suited to take hold of this case. He had little suspicion that he would meet with the severest experience as yet encountered by him and that matters of such a nature would confront him as would tax to the limit his physical endurance. Though this Capuchin Father is the very picture of health in his sixtieth year, yet he needed all available resources in order to carry the affair to a successful finish.

The day agreed upon and approved by the Bishop for the exorcism at Earling, Iowa, was at hand. Besides the pastor and his sister, who was his housekeeper, and the Venerable Sisters, not a soul was aware of what was being undertaken. This secrecy had been strictly agreed upon beforehand. The main purpose of such procedure was chiefly to protect the name of the woman, lest anything of the affair might get out among the people and they might point to her and say : "This is the one who was once possessed by the devil." As she was to travel by train, it was found necessary to inform the personnel of the train. For should something happen on the way, their help would have to be available in case the demoniacal influences should create any disturbance. This caution was not in vain, for the men had their hands full. They, however, did not know what the nature of the disturbance really was. The poor creature herself was only too willing to submit to the ecclesiastical procedure, so that she might be delivered from these terrible molestations. Yet she did not always have the necessary control over herself. She made this known after her delivery. Thus, the very night on which she arrived at the Earling station, she was so enraged over those who were to meet her that she felt like taking hold of them and choking them.

Previous arrangements had been made for Father Theophilus to arrive that same night, but by another route. The pastor took his own auto and went to meet him at the depot. Though the new car was always running in tip-top order, it lacked the usual speed on this trip. Everything possible was tried, yet the car would not make any headway towards the station though no flaw could be found with it. The distance was not even worth mentioning, yet it took two hours for the pastor to arrive at the depot. He excused himself to his guest for causing such a delay and disappointment.

To which the latter replied very calmly: "My dear friend, I was not wrought up about it at all. I would have been much more surprised if everything had gone smoothly. Difficulties will arise; they must be expected to arise. The devil will try his utmost to foil our plans. While waiting I prayed constantly that the evil spirit would not be able to harm you, as I suspected that he would try to interfere with your coming, yea, that he would try to injure you personally." Now the pastor undertsood why his auto had balked. This was to be the beginning of many other unpleasant happenings. After such forebodings the reader can imagine that the missionary entered the car with some misgivings. But he took his precautions. He first blessed the auto with the Sign of the Cross and then seated himself in the rear of the car. During the short ride to the rectory he quietly recited the rosary by himself lest something happen on the way to foil the attempt at exorcism.

The two priests arrived without the slightest trouble. Thank God, the woman also had arrived safely at the Sisters' Convent. With this reassurance the difficult task could begin quietly on the morrow. However, that very night the enemy displayed his true colors. News was soon dispatched from the convent to the rectory next door that the woman caused difficulties from the very start. The well-meaning sister in the kitchen had sprinkled holy water over the food on the tray before she carried the supper to the woman. The devil, however, would not be tricked. The possessed woman was aware at once of the presence of the blessed food and became terribly enraged about it. She purred like a cat, and it was absolutely impossible to make her eat. The blessed food was taken back to the kitchen to be exchanged for unblessed food; otherwise the soup bowls and the plates, might have been crashed through the window. It was not possible to trick her with any blessed or consecrated article ; the very presence of it would bring about such intense sufferings in her as though her very body were encased in glowing coal.

The Decisive Moment Had Arrived

The greater part of the townspeople had gone out into the country to work on their fields on the morrow. All was quiet. Both the pastor and missionary, having offered up Holy Mass in the parish church that morning, went over to the convent where everything in a large room was in readiness for the exorcism. Fortified with the Church's spiritual weapons, they would dislodge Satan from his stronghold in the person of the possessed woman. How long would this process last? It was not to be expected that the devil would leave his victim without a fight. Certainly a few days would pass by before the powers of darkness would give in to the powers of Light, before the devils would let loose the soul redeemed by Christ, and return back to hell. It was well that neither the pastor nor the missionary knew with what kind of horde of evil spirits they would have to do battle.

The woman was placed firmly upon the mattress of an iron bed. Upon the advice of Father Theophilus, her arm-sleeves and her dress were tightly bound so as to prevent any devilish tricks. The strongest nuns were selected to assist her in case anything might happen. There was a suspicion that the devil might attempt attacking the exorcist during the ceremony. Should anything unusual happen, the nuns were to hold the woman quiet upon her bed. Soon after the prescribed prayers of the Church were begun, the woman sank into unconsciousness and remained in that state throughout the period of exorcism. Her eyes were closed up so tightly that no force could open them.

Father Theophilus had hardly begun the formula of exorcism in the name of the Blessed Trinity, in the name of the Father, the Son, and the Holy Ghost, in the name of the Crucified Savior, when a hair-raising scene occurred. With lightning speed the possessed dislodged herself from her bed and from the hands of her guards; and her body, carried through the air, landed high above the door of the room and clung to the wall with a tenacious grip. All present were struck with a trembling fear. Father Theophilus alone kept his peace.

"Pull her down. She must be brought back to her place upon the bed!"

Real force had to be applied to her feet to bring her down from her high position on the wall. The mystery was that she could cling to the wall at all! It was through the powers of the evil spirit, who had taken possession of her body.

Again she was resting upon the mattress. To avoid another such feat, precautions were taken and she was held down tightly with stronger hands.

The exorcism was resumed. The prayers of the Church were continued. Suddenly a loud shrill voice rent the air. The noise in the room sounded as though it were far off, somewhere in a desert. Satan howled as though he had been struck over the head with a club. Like a pack of wild beasts suddenly let loose, the terrifying noises sounded aloud as they came out of the mouth of the possessed woman. Those present were struck with a terrible fear that penetrated the very marrow of their bones.

"Silence, Satan. Keep quiet, you infamous reprobate!"

But he continued to yell and howl as one clubbed and tortured, so that despite the closed windows the noises reverberated throughout the neighborhood.

Awe struck people came running hither and thither: "What is the matter. What is up? Is there someone in the convent being murdered?" Not even a pig stabbed with a butcher knife yells with such shrieking howls as this.

The news travelled through the entire parish like a prairie fire: "At the convent they are trying to drive out the devil from one possessed. „ Larger and smaller groups were filled with terror as they approached the scene of action and heard with their own ears the unearthly noises and howlings caused by the evil spirits. The weaker members of the crowd were unable to endure the continued rage coming from the underworld. It was even more tense for those actually present at the scene, who with their own eyes and ears were witnesses to what was going on before them. The physical condition of the possessed presented such a gruesome sight, because of the distorted members of her body, that it was unbearable. The sisters, even the pastor, could not endure it long. Occasionally they had to leave the room to recuperate in the fresh air, to gain new strength for further attendance at the horrible ordeal. The most valiant and self-composed was Father Theophilus. He had been accustomed to Satan's howling displays and blusterings from experiences with him in previous exorcisms. God seems to have favored him with special gifts and qualities for facing such ordeals. On such occasions, with the permission of the Bishop, he carried a consecrated host in a pyx upon his breast in order to safeguard himself against injuries and direct attacks by the evil one. Several times it happened that he was twisted about, trembling like a fluttering leaf in a whirl-wind.

One may ask: Does Satan dare at all to remain in the presence of the All Holy? How can he endure it? Does he not run off like a whipped cur? All we need to remember is that Satan dared to approach our Lord fasting in the desert. He even dared to take the Savior upon a high pinnacle at Jerusalem; and again he carried Him up on a high mountain top. If he showed himself so powerful then, he has not changed since. On the contrary, the devils living in the possessed displayed various abilities and reactions. Those that hailed from the realm of the fallen angels gave evidence of a greater reserve. They twisted about and howled mournfully in the presence of the Blessed Sacrament, acting like whipped curs who growl and snarl under the pain of the biting lash. Those who were once the active souls of men upon earth and were condemned to hell because of their sinful lives acted differently. They showed themselves bold and fearless, as if they wanted every moment to assail the consecrated Species only to discover that they were powerless. Frothing and spitting and vomiting forth unmentionable excrements from the mouth of the poor creature, they would try to ward off the influence of the exorcist. Apparently they were trying to befoul the consecrated Host in the pyx, but failed in their purpose. It was evidently not granted them to spit upon the All Holy directly. At times they would spout forth torrents of spittle and filth out of the entrails of the helpless woman in order to give vent to their bitter spleen and hatred toward the All Holy One.

You say torrents? Actually those present had to live through some terrible experiences. It was heartrending to see all that came forth from the pitiable creature and often the ordeal was almost unbearable. Outpourings that would fill a pitcher, yes, even a pail, full of the most obnoxious stench were most unnatural. These came in quantities that were humanly speaking impossible to lodge in a normal being. At that the poor creature had eaten scarcely anything for weeks, so that there had been reason to fear she would not survive. At one time the emission was a bowl full of matter resembling vomited macaroni. At another time an even greater measure, having the appearance of sliced and chewed tobacco leaves, was emitted. From ten to twenty times a day this wretched creature was forced to vomit though she had taken at the most only a teaspoonful of water or milk by way of food.

One or More Devils

During this exorcism it was necessary to find out definitely whether the exorcist had to deal with one or more devils. It was also important for the exorcist to insist upon getting control over the person and of dispossessing the devil. On various occasions there were different voices coming out of the woman which indicated that un-numbered spirits were here involved. There were voices that sounded bestial and most unnatural, uttering an inexpressible grief and hatred that no human could reproduce. Again voices were heard that were quite human, breathing an atmosphere of keen suffering and indicating bitter feelings of disappointment. As is common in such experiences, Satan can, through the solemn exorcism of the Church, be forced to speak and to give answer. And, finally, he can also be forced to speak the truth even though he was the father of lies from the very beginning. Naturally he will try to mislead and to sidetrack the exorcist. It is also common experience that Satan at first does his utmost to sidestep the questions with clever witty evasions, direct lies, shrewd simulations.

When Satan was asked in the Name of Jesus, the crucified Savior, whether there were more spirits involved in the possession of the woman, he did not feign in the least, but boastfully admitted that there were a number of them present. As soon as the name of Jesus was mentioned, he began through the woman to foam and howl like a wild raving animal.

This ugly bellowing and howling took place every day and at times it lasted for hours. At other times it sounded as though a horde of lions and hyenas were let loose, then again as the mewing of cats, the bellowing of cattle and the barking of dogs. A complete uproar of different animal noises would also resound. This was at first so taxing on the nerves of those present that the twelve nuns were forced to take turns at assisting in order to save themselves and to have the necessary strength to continue facing the siege.

The exorcist: "In the name of Jesus and His most Blessed Mother, Mary the Immaculate, who crushed the head of the serpent, tell me the truth. Who is the leader or prince among you? What is your name?"

Devil, barking like the hound of hell: "Beelzebub."

Exorcist: "You call yourself Beelzebub. Are you not Lucifer, the prince of the devils?"

Devil: "No, not the prince, the chieftain, but one of the leaders."

Exorcist: "You were therefore not a human being, but you are one of the fallen angels, who with selfish pride wanted to be like unto God?"

Devil with grinning teeth: "Yes, that is so. Ha, how we hate Him!"

Exorcist: "Why are you called Beelzebub if you are not the prince of the devils?"

Devil: "Enough, my name is Beelzebub."

Exorcist: "From the point of influence and dignity you must rank near Lucifer, or do you hail from the lower choir of angels?"

Devil : "I once belonged to the seraphic choir."

Exorcist: "What would you do, if God made it possible for you to atone for your injustice to Him?"

Demoniacal sneering: "Are you a competent theologian?"

Exorcist: "How long have you been torturing this poor woman?"

Devil : "Since her fourteenth year."

Exorcist: "How dared you enter into that innocent girl and torture her like that?"

Sneeringly: "Ha, did not her own father curse us into her?"

Exorcist: "But why did you, Beelzebub, alone take possession of her? Who gave you that permission?"

Devil: "Don't talk so foolishly. Don't I have to render obedience to Satan?"

Exorcist : "Then you are here at the direction and command of Lucifer?"

Devil : "Well, how could it be otherwise?"

Let it be noted too that Father Theophilus addressed the devil in English, German, and again in Latin. And the devil, Beelzebub, and all the other devils, replied correctly in the very same tongues in which they were addressed. Apparently they would have understood any language spoken today and would have answered in it. Sometimes it happened that Father Theophilus, while in, an exhausted state of mind, would make slight mispronunciations in his Latin prayers and words of exorcism. At once Beelzebub would intrude and shriek out: "So and so is right! Dumbbell, you don't know anything!"

Once it happened that Father Theophilus did not catch the words the devil spoke in an inarticulate mumbling voice. So he asked the pastor: "What did he say?" Neither had the pastor

understood the devil.
Then the nuns were interrogated: "What did he say?"

One answered: "So and so, I think."

Then the devil bellowed and yelped at them: "You, I did not say that. Stick to the truth!"

Father Theophilus indeed was anxious to know why the father had cursed his own daughter. But he only received a curt uncivil reply: "You can ask him himself. Let me in peace for once."

Exorcist: "Is then the father of the woman also present as one of the devils? Since when?"

Devil: "What a foolish question. He has been with us ever since he was damned." A terrible sneering laughter followed full of malicious joy.

Exorcist: "Then I solemnly command in the name of the Crucified Savior of Nazareth that you present the father of this woman and that he give me answer!"

A deep rough voice announced itself, which had already been noticed alongside the voice of Beelzebub.

Exorcist: "Are you the unfortunate father who has cursed his own child?"

With a defiant roar: "No."

"Who are you then?"

"I am Judas."

"What, Judas! Are you Judas Iscariot, the former Apostle?"

Thereupon followed a horrible, woefully prolonged: "Y-e-s, I am the one." This was howled in the deepest bass voice. It set the whole room a-quivering so that out of pure fright and horror the pastor and some of the nuns ran out. Then followed a disgusting exhibition of spitting and vomiting as if Judas were intending to spit at his Lord and Master with all his might, or as if he had in mind to unloose his inner waste and filth upon Him.

Finally Judas was asked: "What business have you here?"

"To bring her to despair, so that she would commit suicide and hang herself! She must get the rope, she must go to hell!"

"Is it then a fact that everyone that commits suicide goes to hell?"

"Rather not."

"Why not?"

"Ha, we devils are the ones that urge them to commit suicide, to hang themselves, just as I did myself."

"Do you not regret that you have committed such a despicable deed?"

A terrible curse followed: "Let me alone. Don't bother me with your fake god. It was my own fault." Then he kept on raving in a terrible manner.

The Demon Jacob

When the prayer of exorcism was renewed, the demon Jacob made his appearance with a healthy manly voice. As in the case of Judas, one could detect at once that he had been a human being.

"Which Jacob are you?" asked the exorcist.

"The father of the possessed girl."

Later developments disclosed the fact that he had led a frightfully coarse and brutal life, a passionately unchaste and debased life. He now admitted that he had repeatedly tried to force his own daughter to commit incest with him. But she had firmly resisted him. Therefore he had cursed her and wished inhumanly that the devils would enter into her and entice her to commit every possible sin against chastity, thereby ruining her, body and soul. He also admitted that he did not die suddenly but that he was permitted to receive the sacrament of Extreme Unction. But this was of no avail because he scoffed at and ridiculed the priest ministering the sacrament to him. Later in the exorcism he made the following explanation: Whatever sins he had committed in this life might still have been forgiven him before death, so that he could have been saved; but the crime of giving his own child to the devils was the thing that finally determined his eternal damnation. Even in hell he was still scheming how to torture and molest his child. Lucifer gladly permitted him to do this. And since he was in his own daughter, he was not, despite all the solemn prayers of the Church, in the least disposed to give her up or leave her.

"But you will obey! The power of Christ and the Blessed Trinity will force you back into the pit of hell where you belong!"

Then followed a loud roar and protest: "No, no, only spare me that!"

As the prayers of exorcism were continued, Jacob's mistress, who was in hell with him, also had to face the ordeal and give answer. Her high pitched voice, almost a falsetto, had already been noticed among the many other voices. She now confessed that she was Mina.

Mina admitted that the cause of her damnation was her prolonged immoral life with Jacob while his wife was still living. But a more specific cause for her eternal woes in hell was her unrepented acts of child murder.

Exorcist: "You committed murder while you were still alive? Whom did you kill?"

Mina, bitterly: "Little ones." Evidently she meant her own children.

Exorcist: "How many did you actually kill?"

Mina, most unwillingly curt: "Three — No, actually four!"

Mina showed herself especially hateful. Her replies were filled with such bitter hatred and spite that they far surpassed all that had happened so far. Her demeanor towards the Blessed Sacrament is beyond description. She would spit and vomit in a most hideous manner so that both Father Theophilus and the pastor had to use handkerchiefs constantly to wipe off the spittle from habit and cassock. Because of her unworthy communions, it was clear that the Blessed Sacrament, the Bread of Eternal Life, which should have been the source of her eternal salvation, turned out to be unto her eternal damnation. For she tried to get at the Blessed Sacrament with a burning vengeance and hatred. Out of this group of devils, Mina and Judas were the worst offenders against the Blessed Sacrament.

The reader would undoubtedly be misled if he were of the opinion that these questions and answers followed in regular order. It must be remembered that these battles and encounters with the devils extended over a number of days. At times the answers were interrupted with hours and hours of howling and yelling which could be brought into submission only by prolonged prayer and persistent exorcism. Often no further answers could be forced from the devils in any other way. Countless brats of devils also interrupted the process of exorcism by their disagreeable and almost unbearable interferences. As a result of these disturbances, the woman's face became so distorted that no one could recognize her features. Then, too, her whole body became so horribly disfigured that the regular contour of her body vanished. Her pale, death-like and emaciated head, often assuming the size of an inverted water pitcher, became as red as glowing embers. Her eyes protruded out of their sockets, her lips swelled up to proportions equaling the size of hands, and her thin emaciated body was bloated to such enormous size that the pastor and some of the sisters drew back out of fright, thinking that the woman would be torn to pieces and burst asunder. At times her abdominal regions and extremities became as hard as iron and stone. In such instances the weight of her body pressed into the iron bedsteads so that the iron beams of the bed bent to the floor.

According to the prescribed formula of the Church, the solemn exorcism began with the recitation of the Litany of All Saints. All those present knelt and answered the prayers. At first the evil spirits remained peaceful, but when the petitions, "God the Father of heaven", "God the Son Redeemer of the World," "God the Holy Ghost", "Holy Trinity one God," were said, the regular turmoil and gnashing of teeth began. At the petitions, "Holy Mary," "St. Michael," the devils subsided as if struck by a bolt of lightning. A murmuring and muffled groaning arose at the mention of the Choir of Angels and the Holy Apostles. At the words: "From the persecution of the devil," the evil spirit jumped up as if a scourge had hit him.

"From the spirit of uncleanliness," how he squirmed! "Through Thy Cross and Passion," how he moaned and yelped like a beaten cur!

Acute Cause of the Devil's Pain

As the exorcism progressed, one could see that the benediction of the Blessed Sacrament pained the devil most acutely. That was always something unbearable for him. How he spat and vomited! He twisted and raved at the blessing with the Relic of the Cross. Whenever the priest approached him with the cross and the prescribed words, "Look at the wood of the cross! Begone ye powers of hell! The lion of the tribe of Judah shall conquer," he acted terribly.

"Stop it, stop it, I cannot bear it, I cannot listen to it !" he seemed to say.

And when the exorcist approached him with the relic of the cross hidden under his cassock, Satan became a raving maniac. "Begone, begone," he howled, "I cannot bear it. Oh, this is torture! It is unbearable !"

The intercession, "Mary, the Immaculate Conception", caused him fearful agony. When he was addressed, "I command you in the name of the Immaculate Conception, in the name of her who crushed the head of the serpent", he wilted and languished. Then he bloated up the woman's body, and suddenly relaxed as one stunned.

Holy Water

Holy Water was also something hateful to Satan. Whenever he was approached with holy water he screamed: "Away, away with it, away with that abominable dirt! Oh, that burns, that scorches!" On one occasion a piece of paper bearing the inscription of a fake Latin prayer was placed on the woman's head. Even the good nuns believed that the prayer was genuine. In reality, the prayer consisted of words taken out of a pagan classic. The nuns were very much surprised that Satan remained so quiet under the experiment. The exorcist, however, knew the cause of the devil's tranquility. Immediately afterwards, a second prepared paper was placed on the head of the woman, which had been blessed beforehand with the sign of the cross and holy water without anybody noticing it. In an instant the piece of paper was torn into a thousand shreds.

Little Flower of the Child Jesus

The pastor had kept a small relic of the Little Flower of the Child Jesus in his sacristy in a small pyx without the knowledge of Father Theophilus. For protection's sake, he placed this in a side-pocket of his cassock one day and entered the convent where the exorcism was taking place. Just as the pastor entered the room, the devil began to rave: "Away, away with that! Away with the relic of the Little Flower, away with that weathercock!"

"We have no relic of the Little Flower," the exorcist exclaimed.

"Certainly, he who just entered has one," said the devil, indicating the pastor. At the same time the pastor approached with the relic. How the devil began to spit and to resist!

At other times the Little Flower played a more important part. One could also notice what a terrific battle Satan had with St. Michael.

St. Michael

At the very mention of St. Michael Satan began to recoil. He was tortured by that part of the prayer which refers to the solemn petition in behalf of St. Michael. He absolutely refused to listen to the statement that St. Michael, as leader of the faithful angels, cast Lucifer together with his legions into the very abyss of hell. It was astounding how much he dreaded the prayer in honor of St. Michael commonly recited at the end of the Mass. The prayer is as follows:

"St. Michael the Archangel, defend us in battle. Be our safeguard against the wickedness and destruction of the devil. Restrain him 0 God, we humbly beseech Thee, and do thou, 0 Prince of the heavenly host, by the power of God cast him into hell with the other evil spirits, who prowl about the world seeking the ruin of souls. Amen."

Would that we as Christians recited this prayer in honor of St. Michael with greater fervor and devotion.

Crucifix and Relic of the Cross

A rather peculiar circumstance induced Pope Leo XIII to compose this powerful prayer. After celebrating Mass one day he was in conference with the Cardinals. Suddenly he sank to the floor. A doctor was summoned and several came at once. There was no sign of any pulse beating, the very life seemed to have ebbed away from the already weakened and aged body. Suddenly he recovered and said : "What a horrible picture I was permitted to see!" He saw what was going to happen in the future, the misleading powers and the ravings of the devils against the Church in all countries. But St. Michael had appeared in the nick of time and cast Satan and his cohorts back into the abyss of hell. Such was the occasion that caused Pope Leo XIII to have this prayer recited over the entire world at the end of the Mass. As indicated before, Satan dreaded the Sign of the Cross, a crucifix, or a relic of the true cross. On one occasion a crucifix not made of wood was handed to Father Theophilus. This time Satan broke out in a sneering and ridiculing laughter : "Ha, so you arrived with a pasteboard cross ! Since when did 'He* die on a paper cross? If my knowledge doesn't fail me, He was nailed to a wooden cross."

The crucifix was examined more closely and was indeed found to be made not of wood but of papier-mache. On another occasion Satan made fun of the manner in which Christ was nailed to the cross. "Were not the feet of Jesus nailed one on top of the other, and not aside of each other"? Catherine Emmerich gives the same information. She says that the left foot was nailed first with a shorter nail. Then a longer and stronger nail, at the sight of which our Savior is said to have shuddered, was driven first through the right foot and then through the left. Those standing nearby at the crucifixion saw very plainly how the nail penetrated both feet.

This does not mean that we are now sure how the feet of our Savior were placed upon the cross, even if Beelzebub's statement tends to confirm the description given by Catherine Emmerich. We do not give the father of lies credit for being a reliable witness in such matters as the crucifixion even if there is no doubt that many devils were personal witnesses to the crucifixion of Christ. In like manner I would have no one believe that we know for certain that Judas is in hell, just because he appeared in person as one of the damned in the case of possession at Earling. Holy Mother Church has never yet given a decision regarding this matter even though the words of our Savior about Judas are thought-provoking: "It would have been better if that man had never been born."

As the days passed by, a rather odd experience manifested itself in the disposition of the pastor who began to experience a rather strong antipathy against the whole procedure of driving out the devil.

Antipathy Against The Whole Procedure

The pastor could no longer bear the presence of Father Theophilus who had been a dear friend of his all along, and whom he had known intimately for years. If he would only be out of the way, out of sight! He now wished that he had refused to allow this exorcism to be performed in his parish, and that he had sent him directly out of his house. He became so worked up about it that he finally informed the exorcist of his ill-feeling toward him and the whole affair. Father Th. did not show the least surprise. The case was still in the developing stages and it was only natural to suppose that the devil would have recourse to some source of temptation and annoyance in order to foil all attempts at dislodging him from the one possessed.

Furthermore, the devil used every occasion to display his hatred for the pastor. "You are the cause of the whole affair, you are the one who tortures us so painfully," he burst out. The exorcist commanded Satan on one occasion as follows: "Be quiet, you hellish serpent. Let the pastor in peace once for all. He is not harming you in the least. I am doing this with the powers of exorcism."

This riled the devil all the more. He said: "It is the pastor ! He is at fault. Had he not given you permission to use his church and convent, you wouldn't be able to do a thing. And even today you would be helpless against us, if he would retract his assent."

This is an interesting proof of how the devil feels about and recognizes authority. He made this evident to every superior, while he acted rather civilly towards the subordinates. For that reason he never attacked the nuns nor the pastor's cook. All that the pastor or the mother superior had to do was to appear on the scene and the disturbance and raving was on. The mother superior once received such a blow across the face that she was thrust into the corner of the room.

Satan repeatedly threatened Father Steiger, the pastor :

"You will have to suffer for that."

"You can't harm me anyway. I am standing under the protection of Almighty God, and against His power you are absolutely helpless, you detestable hell-hound."

"Just wait ! I'll make you repent that. I'll incite the whole parish against you and I will calumniate you in such a way that you will no longer be able to defend yourself. Then you will have to pack up and leave in shame and regret."

"If that be the will of God, then God be praised! But you are powerless against Him, you vile serpent, you man killer!"

"Just wait! I will fix both you and your Lord and Master."

"Ha, how dare you speak that way against the Almighty, you despicable worm crawling in the very dust of the earth!"

"No, I cannot harm God directly. But I can touch you and His Church." And he continued with scorn and sarcasm: "Is it not true? Do you not know the history of Mexico? We have prepared a nice mess for Him there."

"Who? You devils?"

"Who else did it? The whole credit is ours for bringing that situation about. He will learn to know us better. Lucifer is on His tracks and will make the kettle hot and heavy for Him. Ha, ha, ha!"

A week later the devil advanced a little closer with his plans of revenge upon the pastor.

"Just wait", he threatened, "until the end of the week! When Friday comes, then..."

The pastor did not take this threat to heart. He was getting sick of listening to the howlings and yelpings of the devil day after day.

Yet the pastor did indeed have a narrow escape on a certain Friday.

The Experience of His Life

Friday morning after Mass the telephone rang in the parish house. It was a call from a farmer, whose mother was critically ill. Would the pastor kindly come and administer the last sacraments to the dying? He wanted to call for the pastor with his own car, but somehow it was out of order and he couldn't locate the trouble. He had been trying to start it for over an hour, but in vain. It simply would not start. So he asked the pastor to come with his own auto, or to hire a taxi at the farmer's expense.

Within a quarter of an hour the pastor was on his way to help the sick woman, carrying the Blessed Sacrament with him. After dispensing the last sacraments, Father Steiger was again on the road towards Earling. The road was familiar to him, for he had gone that way hundreds of times, by night and by day, and he knew every bump and stone along the way. He drove very carefully not only because the auto was new, but also because he was mindful of the devil's threats to trick him whenever the opportunity was ripe.

He prayed to his Guardian Angel and to St. Joseph, his Patron Saint, for a safe journey home. Suddenly as he was driving along, a dense black cloud appeared before him. It came just as he was about to pass a bridge over a deep ravine. Great God, it seemed as if his eyes were blindfolded! The next moment there was a crash, a smash-up which dumbfounded him. He found himself in a mess of ruins. The auto had crashed into the railing of the bridge with an indescribable force although he had jerked the car into low gear. The auto, now a complete wreck, was hanging on the iron trellis threatening every moment to drop into the deep abyss below. The noice of the crash was so loud that a farmer ploughing a field some distance away heard the noise and became greatly alarmed. Full of anxiety he hastened to the scene of the accident. Good God, it's the pastor's car! "Father, Father, what happened? Are you hurt?" The pastor, scared to death, slowly crawled out from underneath the debris. Even the steering wheel was crushed to pieces. His legs would hardly hold him up. The wonder of it was that the rod of the steering wheel had not pierced his breast as frequently happens in such accidents. The farmer hastened home at once and reappeared with his own car. Leaving the wrecked car behind, he took the pastor, still shaking and in a deathlike pallor, into his own car and hurried directly to the nearest doctor to ascertain if there were any internal injuries. No, he was not seriously injured. The doctor discovered some external scars and a state of nervous excitement, but there was no sign of any internal injury. Thank God for that!

Leaving the doctor's office, they drove straight to the parish house at Earling. There was no one at home, for they had all gone over to the convent to witness the exorcism. So the pastor also went there. He had hardly entered the room when he was greeted with a roaring laughter full of vengeance and bitter spleen: "Hahaha— hahaha!" as if the devil were about to burst into a fit of malicious joy at besting him. "Today he pulled in his proud neck and was outpointed! I certainly showed him up today. What about your new auto, that dandy car which was smashed to smitherenes? It served you right!"

The others looked wonderingly at the pastor. He was still pale but nothing ailed him otherwise.

"Reverend Pastor, is the devil speaking the truth?" they asked.

"Yes, what he says is true. My auto is a complete wreck. But he was not able to harm me personally."

A quick reply came from the devil: "Our aim was to get you, but somehow our plans were thwarted. It was your powerful Patron Saint who prevented us from harming you."

News of this accident soon spread abroad and the people in deep sympathy with their beloved pastor, collected enough money to buy him a new car, so that the devil would receive no satisfaction from his pranks. Again and again the devil gleefully reminded the pastor of this incident and warned him to "be ready for a whole lot more fun."

The devil also betrayed himself by saying that he is often the cause of similar accidents in order to bring people to quicker ruin. In that way he can get his revenge and give vent to his anger because lawsuits frequently result as a consequence, which, in turn, are responsible for much hatred and misunderstanding among people.

The reader may make his own conclusions and resolutions regarding this. It cannot be so readily denied that the enemy of mankind actually plays a great part in such accidents. Is he not a "mankiller from the very beginning?" Hence a timely warning to those who use the auto for evil purposes, who decorate it with all sorts of nonsense and who even display figures alluringly immoral. The Church has provided a special blessing under the protection of St. Christopher against evil and disastrous influences. Therefore, it is customary to put one of these beloved medals or medallions in every car for safety's sake. St. Paul calls attention to the fact that the very air is filled with evil spirits.

Satan's Speeches

It should be noted that Satan did not use the tongue of the poor possessed woman to make himself understood. The helpless creature had been unconscious during the greater part of the trial. Her mouth was closed tight. Even when it was open there was not the slightest movement of the lips, nor were there any changes in the position of the mouth. The evil spirits simply spoke in an audible manner from somewhere within her. Possibly they used some inner organ of the body.

We know from the early Christian writers of the Roman period that the heathens frequently heard voices coming out of their idols. Catherine Emmerich also states that the evil spirits took up their abode in these idols and could clearly be heard to speak from within them in order to confirm the heathens in their delusion of idolatry. So it is conceivable how even some of the highly educated heathens worshipped these statues made by the hands of man, and why they offered sacrifices to them as if they were gods. They rendered to these idols the honor that belongs to God alone.

Satan's Knowledge Can Be Embarrassing

The knowledge Satan had about the sins and the condition of the souls of those present was rather embarrassing to them. But in this case there were no disturbing revelations made along that line as there were only nuns and priests present. But even here he made insinuating remarks: "It is not true that you did so and so in your past life, in your childhood days?" He made reference here to acts which were hardly remembered. The evil spirit, however, would not be quiet and tried to make a scene of things. So the answer was given him: "If before God I am not guilty of greater faults in my later years than the sins of my childhood days, then I am not afraid."

Thereupon followed a most astonishing confession from the devil:

"WHAT YOU HAVE ALREADY CONFESSED, I DO NOT KNOW"

What follows from this? Apparently Satan knows only the sins that have not been confessed or repented. What has been submitted to the keys of the confessional seems to be out of his reach. It would seem that the sacrament of penance blots out or obliterates sins from the soul so as not to leave the slightest possibility for Satan to discover them. Through the sacrament of penance everything is, so to say, drowned in the abyss of God's mercy.

The rubrics in the Roman Ritual for exorcism, so wisely and so well established, demand that not only the exorcist, but also all witnesses and all those called upon to aid in subduing the possessed person, should make a thorough general confession, or at least a sincere act of perfect contrition before the process of exorcism begins. Once cleansed from sin they are more at ease in facing Satan and will not be subject to annoying remarks on the part of Satan for the sins committed in the past.

It happened about forty years ago in a case of possession at Wemding, Germany, that during the process of exorcism the mistake was made of calling in the strongest men of the parish, men of good repute, to subdue a raving young boy. These good men did not realize with whom they had to deal. The horrible beastlike howling and yelping was far less disconcerting than the hair-raising reproofs of the devil for the secret sins and other mistakes of one or the other of these men. He described them in minutest detail. Under such circumstances it is not surprising that few people care to be present at such an exorcism, even if they could make themselves useful in many ways. Furthermore, it must be remembered that Satan, the father of lies, often twists small acts into unusually and seemingly grievous ones, making mountains out of molehills, so to speak, and at times purposely distorting them, mixing up truth with falsehood with the intention of creating the greatest disorder and most lasting enmity.

In order to avoid such inconvenient consequences, Father Theophilus, richer by mature experiences, undertakes his exorcism in consecrated or religious houses with only the assistance of priests and nuns. Even then things have happened. Satan shrewdly and sagaciously disclosed hidden things which made certain persons blush for shame; yea, he made them quiver with fear by threatening to expose them still more. All the more fortunate, then, that such experience that will henceforth take place under the seal of secrecy and will not be broadcast to the whole world. Thank God for that!

The meanness of the devil and the many odd happenings at Earling became common knowledge among the people in the bordering communities. The pastor of Earling, Father Steiger, had asked his people to unite in prayer and penance, and to make visits to the Blessed Sacrament so that the evil spirit might soon be mastered. Despite common knowledge of the unusual proceedings going on at the convent, not a single person asked out of curiosity to be permitted to witness the scene. Even if anyone had asked, permission would not have been granted, except to priests from the neighborhood.

It has been intimated above that out of the voices coming from the possessed woman, four different ones could be very clearly distinguished. They announced themselves as Beelzebub, Judas Iscariot, Jacob, the father of the possessed woman, and Mina,

Jacob's concubine.

The possessed woman had a clear memory of when her godless father cursed her and handed her over to the devil. She did not mention any further details about her unfortunate father, but it was learned from other sources that he was one of the worst persecutors of priests and of the Church. In sensual lust and excesses he was a monster of the worst type. He kept his distance from the Church and her sacramental ministration, and used every opportunity to ridicule spiritual things. Occasionally, he attended divine services on solemn feast days, but only to acquire new material from the sermons or the solemn functions to feed his ridicule and so bolster up his criticisms among friends and companions. Hence we can understand how he persisted in ridiculing the priest and his actions when, even in his last moments, a merciful God granted him the grace of receiving the last sacrament of Extreme Unction. As you live, so you die. And his concubine, Mina, was fully his equal in this respect. Birds of a feather flock together.

What was most surprising was that such a wicked and blasphemous father was blessed with such a virtuous child. Her sincere piety, her pure and innocent disposition, her diligent application, all were very apparent. Even during the period of possession the devil could not disturb her inner basic disposition because the devil has no power over the free will of a human being.

It was evident that, in addition to the above mentioned devils, there were also a great number of other unclean spirits in her. Among these the so-called dumb devils and avenging spirits made themselves especially prominent.

Dumb Devils
and Avenging Spirits

The number of silent devils was countless. Apparently they were from the lower classes, for they displayed no marks of strength or power. Their voices were rather a confusion of sounds from which no definite answers could be distinguished. There was no articulate, speech, rather a pitiful moaning and subdued howling. They could put up little resistance against the powerful effects of exorcism. It seemed as though they came and left in hordes, one crowd being relieved by others of the same type. They reminded one of a traveler who is suddenly overtaken by a swarm of mosquitoes. A few puffs of tobacco drive them away, but in short order they return and pester him again.

Avenging Spirits

The avenging spirits were wild and violent, of rough and ill-mannered character. They were filled with hatred and anger against all human beings. Their very presence suggested an ugly and disgusting attitude — a mixture of hatred and envy, meanness and revenge, deception and trickery. These were precisely the ones that threatened to make the pastor rue his consent to this exorcism. They had in mind to stir up the whole parish against him by their misrepresentations, so that he would have to pack up and leave in disgust. One might presume from this that the devils are much to blame for bringing about misunderstandings between the pastor and the people. Not infrequently pastors tell of how they sacrificed themselves, even ruined their health, for the good of the people, but despite all their untiring efforts, some of the most inconceivable misinterpretations and misrepresentations had taken place in their parishes. Some people seem to find it their business to make the life of their shepherd so miserable that he is brought almost to the point of despair. All his good intentions bring him nothing, but persecutions of the worst sort. Hence it would not be amiss for pastors to use the small formula of exorcism periodically in order to protect their flocks from such meddlings of the devil, or to use the prayers composed by Pope Leo XIII for just such an emergency.

The scheming and plotting of these avenging spirits almost succeeded in inciting the pastor of Earling to white heat against Father Th., his friend of long standing, doubtless with the intention of preventing the success of the exorcism. He was so wrought up over the procedure at times that he thought of bringing the whole affair to an abrupt close by driving Father Theophilus from his church and convent with the sharpest words of reproof.

Night Prowlers

During the process of exorcism, the evil spirits repeatedly made statements to the effect that they would tire and exhaust the pastor. One time in the middle of the night he was suddenly awakened by a disturbance in the room. Were rats gnawing somewhere? It seemed to be between the walls near his bed. Was there so much room there that the rats could run about so freely? During his fourteen years in this same house he had never experienced anything of the kind. Was he to be bothered with such miserable pests at last? He pounded the wall with his fist to scare away the rodents. But to no avail. He first used his cane, then his shoe, to pound on the wall. Instead of letting up, the noise became worse. Perhaps the night prowlers would disappear of their own accord. He waited and waited. They continued up and down between the walls, and even threatened to ruin them.

Father Steiger was in need of a good night's rest after all the disturbances during the day. An idea came that seemed altogether too foolish. Could there be some relation between these night prowlers and the evil spirits of the exorcism? Had not the devils threatened to tire him out? Perhaps this is what they meant after all. If so, then there is only one thing to do, and that is to use spiritual weapons against these intruders. Fortifying himself with his stola, the pastor again tried to sleep. At last, the noise let up, but not altogether. "Wait, you cursed hellrats, I'll get rid of you yet!" Getting up again, he lit two candles before a crucifix and recited the small formula of exorcism against evil spirits. Aha! That was the language these hellrats understood. They took to flight and all was quiet. They seemed to have been spirited, blown off now, although all previous thumping and pounding on the walls had brought no results.

A few nights thereafter the pastor again spent a restless night. Are the doors rattling? Is the house quaking? Oh, it's only a heavy express train going through the village, and these noises are only the after rumblings of the jarred earth. The railroad track was only a short distance away. He waited for the train to start from the depot, but he heard no move. Perhaps it's the rattling of machinery in the nearby electric shop!

Finally, the noise ceased. But suddenly it was heard again, this time right above the door. Maybe the door is ajar so that a draft is swaying it back and forth. There was no door stop to catch it, and so he had to get up again. But lo! the door was closed firmly. He took hold of the knob with a firm grip and pulled hard ; it did not yield. What, is the devil again at his pranks to tire him out, to rob him of his night's rest? The pastor took the holy water, sprinkled the door, windows, and room, and recited the short formula of exorcism. Again all was quiet. There was not a stir after that. "O you miserable Satan, now I know your stealthly cunning. Just wait, I'll soon teach you good manners."

It was learned later that other priests, who had attended the process of expelling the devil, experienced similar inconveniences and annoyances. Even worse things had happened to them. They would not retire after that without having holy water and the stola with them. The noises were often so persistent that one or the other of the priests was obliged to get up at night and seek the place and cause of the disturbances, and only after praying was he able to find peace again. Night prowlers of this kind have been met with in other cases of exorcism even long after the evil spirits had been driven out of the possessed person.

How the Possessed Woman Fared

Every day the woman lost consciousness and became utterly helpless shortly after the formula of exorcism had begun. When the exercises ceased, she woke up and was herself again. She declared that she was unaware of what transpired during the exercises. Quite exhausted, she had to be carried to and from the place where the exorcism was performed. During all this time she could not eat solid foods, but nourishment in liquid form was injected into her. It was surprising to note how such a weak creature could vomit forth such quantities of material as indicated above. It was not unusual for her to vomit twenty to thirty times a day.

The fact that, in her weakened condition, she could bear up under the daily strain of exorcism for three weeks seems incredible, especially when the terrible abuses upon her body inflicted by the devil, are taken into consideration. She suffered so intensely on one occasion that she assumed a death-like color, and seemed ready to pass away at any moment. "Great God, she is dying. I will hasten to get the holy oils!" broke out the pastor, who realized the terrible consequences for all concerned if she died under these conditions. The charge that the priests had caused her death through the strain of exorcism would certainly have been launched against them. Father Theophilus calmly replied on the basis of his long experience: "Just remain here, my friend; the woman will not die. Absolutely not.

This manifestation is only one of Satan's cunning tricks. He cannot and will not be permitted to kill her. Absolutely not."

Exorcism Lasted Twenty-Three Days

The period of exorcism extended over an unusually long period of time. Never before did it take so long, as far as we know. It lasted just twenty-three days. And remember, the exorcism went on from early morning until late night. The devil tried his utmost to weaken the priests and nuns and to induce them to let up in their untiring efforts. The pastor could not always be present. His care of souls in the parish kept him away at times. Neither was he physically able to sacrifice so many hours of the night for this purpose. Thus it happened that many interesting and also terrible things took place in his absence to which, however, the others were trustworthy witnesses.

The solemn formula of exorcism was in progress for more than two w r eeks before there were any indications that the devil could be forced to depart from the poor helpless possessed woman. Even though Father Theophilus had succeeded in delivering her from a large number of devils through the great powers of the prayers and exorcisms, the four meanest and most persistent ones could not be dislodged for a long time. Satan seemed to have gathered up all the forces of hell to gain a final victory in this case.

High Commander

It was very evident that the forces of hell were under the direction of a high commander who, like a general and field marshall, sent forth new recruits for battle whenever the veterans, in their exhausted condition, were forced to retire. What pitiful sighs and pleadings they sent forth. One could hear voices to this effect: "Oh, what we have to put up with here; it is just terrible, all that we have to suffer." There were other voices that kept on urging their fellow-devils not to let up: "And how we will again have to suffer and cringe under him, how he will torture us again if we return without having accomplished our task." They clearly referred to Lucifer as the torturer.

In order not to give Satan and his hordes any peace whatever, Father Theophilus finally decided to continue the exorcisms himself throughout the night, expecting thereby to achieve his victory. He was blessed with a muscular body and with nerves of steel. He had tested these out by a rigorous and abstemious life of self-denial, which had given him great powers of endurance. And indeed it was something almost superhuman that was demanded of him. For three days and three nights he kept on without any intermission. Even the sisters who alternated were on the verge of a breakdown. Yet the desired effect did not come. It was only with the summoning of his last strength that the exorcist dared to continue. And at the close of the twenty-third day he was completely spent. He had the appearance of a walking corpse, a figure which at any moment might collapse. His own countenance seemed to have aged twenty years during those three weeks.

Antichrist

The reader may at this time be inclined to ask if the devil disclosed things that would be of general interest. For instance, the question of the Antichrist. What did Satan have to say about him?

It must be clearly borne in mind that the questions directed to the devil and the answers given by him were by no means an entertaining dialogue between the evil spirits and the exorcist. On occasions a long time intervened before an answer could be forced out of Satan. For the greater part, only a ghastly bellowing, groaning and howling was the result, whenever he was urged to answer under the powers of exorcism. It was often such a terrible drudgery, so exhaustingly tiresome and irritating, that on some days the exorcist was completely covered with perspiration. He had to make a complete change of attire as often as three to four times a day. Towards the end of those terrible days he became so weak, that he felt he could continue only with the special help of God. Yes, he even pleaded for the grace to be spared his own life. Curious questions not related to the present exorcism were never purposely asked. At times, however, it happened that some of the answers given by the devil himself suggested other questions not strictly pertinent to the case.

On such occasions, Father Theophilus was snubbed by the devil with coarse and harsh replies: "Shut up, that is none of your business!" Satan often used the crisp Latin expression: "Non ad rem!" Which means, "not to the point," "that has nothing to do with this affair."

At one time Satan became rather talkative about the Antichrist. Remember the time he had so triumphantly referred to the Mexican situation, when he said that he would stir up a fine mess for Him (Jesus) and His Church, far more detrimental than hitherto. When asked whether he meant that the furious rage of the Antichrist would be directed against the Church of God, he asserted that that was, self-evident and insolently continued: "Yes, Satan is already abroad, and the Antichrist is already born in Palestine. (On another occasion he also mentioned America.) But he is still young. He must first grow up incognito before his power can become known."

In another case of possession the devil gave the years 1952-55 as the time of the Antichrist's appearance.

It is strange that Catherine Emmerich mentioned a similar period, when she gave a description of Christ's descent into hell after His death upon the cross. She related that "when the portals of hell were opened by the angels, there was a terrible uproar, cursing, scolding, howling and moaning. Individual angels were hurling hordes of evil spirits aside. All were commanded to adore Jesus. This caused them the greatest pain. In the center of it all there was a bottomless abyss as black as night. Lucifer was bound in chains and cast into this depth of darkness. All this happened in accordance with set laws. I heard that Lucifer, if I am not mistaken, would again be freed for a time about fifty or sixty years before the year 2000 A.D. A number of other devils would be released somewhat earlier as a punishment and source of temptation to sinful human beings."

On one occasion, when Father Th. insisted that the devil should depart and return to hell, the devil replied in a growling tone: "How can you banish me to hell? I must be free to prepare the way for the Anti-christ." And again he spoke out of the possessed woman: "We know a lot. We read the signs of the times. This is the last century. When people will write the year 2000 the end will be at hand."

Whether the "father of lies", as our Lord Himself styles Satan, spoke the truth, it is impossible to judge. At all events, we shall do well if according to our Lord's suggestion, we try to understand the signs of the times.. That the powers of hell are putting up a desperate attempt to ruin the Church of Christ in our own times cannot be denied.

At one time the evil spirits howled and yelped fearfully when the prayers of exorcism were solemnly pronounced and when the blessings with the relic of the cross and the consecrated Host were given: "Oh, we cannot bear it any longer. We suffer intensely. Do stop it, do stop it! This is many times worse than Hell. These groans, indicating the attendant pain and suffering, cut to the quick.

"Therefore, depart at once, ye cursed! It is entirely within your power to free yourselves from these sufferings. Let this poor woman in peace! I conjure you in the name of the Almighty God, in the name of the Crucified Jesus of Nazareth, in the name of His purest Mother, the Virgin Mary, in the name of the Archangel Michael!"

"Oh, yes," they groaned, "we are willing. But Lucifer does not let us."

"Tell the truth. Is Lucifer alone the cause of it?"

"No, he alone could not be. God's justice does not permit it as yet, because sufficient atonement has not yet been made for her."

This admission was valuable. It offered a greater inducement to arouse the members of the parish to increase their acts of expiation for the woman.

More Atonement

In accordance with the request of their pastor, the parishioners gladly went to church to keep regular hours of adoration before the Blessed Sacrament. They prayed fervently for the destruction of the powers of Satan, and for the victory of the Church in delivering the victim from the tenacious grip of the devil. Following the directions of the ritual, the pastor kept on encouraging his people to private fasting and penance in order that their petitions would be more effective in strengthening the prayers of the exorcism. Our Lord Himself, when putting the devil to flight, and after beseeching all to pray, had told the Apostles that this kind of devils can only be driven away by prayers and fasting. The devil's own statement, that sufficient penance had not been done, helped to bring about more fervent prayers and more rigorous penances. The faithful flocked to church in large numbers from early morn until late in the evening in order that, by their prayers, they might add their mite to the work of the Church in this her mission. The exorcism could not continue much longer as the reserve strength of those actually assisting was being vitally sapped.

Battles Between Good and Evil Spirits

It was during this time that the poor woman admitted during her periods of rest that she had visions of horrible battles between the good and evil spirits. Countless numbers of evil spirits continually arrived. Satan tried his utmost not to be outdone this time. The good angels came to assist at the exorcism. Many approached seated on white horses (Apocalypse 19, 15) and, under the leadership of St. Michael, completely routed the infernal serpents and drove the demons back to the abyss of hell.

The Little Flower of the Child Jesus

The Little Flower of Jesus also appeared to the woman during these crucial days and spoke these consoling words to her: "Do not lose courage! The pastor especially should not give up hope. The end is soon at hand."

This occurred on a certain evening when, to their surprise, the nuns and the pastor's sister suddenly noticed a cluster of white roses on the ceiling. After a while the vision gradually disappeared. The pastor noticed the anxious gaze of these ladies directed towards the ceiling, but he himself did not see the flowers.

The words of encouragement from the Little Flower gave a new impetus to the priests. Now they knew that victory was not far off. During the latter days the devils betrayed great fear lest they be forced to return to hell. Father Th. insisted upon their departure again and again. They pleaded pitifully: "Anything but that, anything but that." To be banished to another place, or into another creature would have been more bearable. They did not want to be driven back to hell.

"But you are already in hell."

"True, true," they groaned, "we drag hell along with us. Yet it is a relief to be permitted to roam about the earth until (at the last judgment) we shall be cast off and damned to hell for eternity."

The Devils Depart

Gradually the resistance of the devils began to wane. They seemed to become more docile. Their bold, bitter demeanor gave way to more moaning and despairing tones. They could not bear the tortures of exorcism any longer. With great uneasiness they explained that they would finally return to hell. But how often they are deceptive and unreliable! Experience teaches us that at times they pretend to leave the possessed entirely at ease for a while, in order to sidetrack the unwary observer and thus outwit him.

For this reason Father Th., almost completely exhausted, demanded in the name of the Most Blessed Trinity that at their departure the devils should give a sign of their leavetaking from the possessed woman by giving their respective names.

"Are you going to do that?"

"Yes," they promised emphatically.

It was on the twenty-third day of September, 1928, in the evening about nine o'clock that, with a sudden jerk of lightning speed the possessed woman broke from the grip of her protectors and stood erect before them. Only her heels were touching the bed. At first sight it appeared as if she were to be hurled up to the ceiling. "Pull her down! Pull her down" called the pastor while Father Th. blessed her with the relic of the cross, saying: "Depart ye fiends of hell! Begone Satan, the Lion of Juda reigns!"

At that very moment the stiffness of the woman's body gave way and she fell upon the bed. Then a piercing sound filled the room causing all to tremble vehemently. Voices saying, "Beelzebub, Judas, Jacob, Mina," could be heard. And this was repeated over and over until they faded far away into the distance.

"Beelzebub, — Judas, — Jacob, — Mina." To these words were added: "Hell, — hell, — hell! „

Everyone present was terrified by this gruesome scene. It was the long awaited sign indicating that Satan was forced to leave his victim at last and to return to hell with his associates.

What a happy sight it was that followed; the woman opened her eyes and mouth for the first time, something that had never taken place while the exorcism itself was going on. She displayed a kindly smile as if she wanted to say: "From what a terrible burden have I been freed at last!"

For the first time in twelve years she uttered the most holy name of Jesus with child-like piety: "My Jesus Mercy! Praised be Jesus Christ!"

Tears of joy filled her eyes and those of all in attendance.

Amid the first rejoicings, the witnesses were not aware of the terrible odor that filled the room. All the windows had to be opened. The stench was unearthly, simply unbearable. It was the last souvenir of the infernal devils who had had to abandon their earthly victim.

What a day of joy it was for the whole parish! *Te Deum lauda-*

mus! Holy God we praise Thy name! Not unto us, not unto us, 0 Lord, but to Thy name be glory and praise.

From that time on the woman, always sincerely good, pious and religious, frequently visited the Blessed Sacrament and assisted at Holy Mass. She received Communion in a most edifying manner. That which was so terrible for her while she was under the torturing powers of Satan is now the peaceful joy of her heart and soul.

Theresa Neumann

Theresa Neumann of Konnersreuth was also concerned in this affair.

Bishop Eis of Switzerland, who had been well informed about the above case, paid a visit to Theresa Neumann. And since it was Friday, he asked her while she was in one of her ecstatic visions whether she was aware of the terrible case of demoniacal pos- session in America. She immediately answered:

"Is it not so? You mean the case in Earling, Iowa, at which some priests scoffed, and about which others were indifferent?"

Then followed an astounding announcement:

"The good woman will later again be possessed. This will be for her own personal benefit, for her own purification and complete atonement."

Furthermore, the stigmatic woman of Konnersreuth had a terrible vision on the Feast of St. Michael, pertaining to the exorcism that had taken place in Earling. She witnessed the frightful battle between the angels of heaven under the leadership of St. Michael and the infernal demons under the command of Lucifer. She was so shocked and confused by it that she said:

"If it be not against the will of God, I will ask Him never again to permit me to witness anything so terrible."

It was by far the worst vision she had ever experienced.

Father Theophilus, basing his opinion on his numerous experiences with cases of possession, believes that the hour of the Antichrist is not far distant. Lucifer himself was present for about fourteen days in the Earling case. With all the forces of hell at his disposal he tried his utmost to make this a test case. Once Father Th. saw Lucifer standing visibly before him for half an hour — a fiery being in his characteristically demoniac reality. He had a crown on his head and carried a fiery sword in his hand.

Beelzebub stood alongside of him. During this time the whole room was filled with flames. Lucifer was cursing and blaspheming in a terrible rage:

"If only I could, I would have choked you long ago. If I only had my former powers, you would soon experience what I could do to you."

Through the powers of Christ he had been deprived of his original might as even now through exorcism his influence was further diminished. Father Th. asked him one time: "What can you accomplish, you helpless Lucifer?"

To which he replied : "What could you do, if you were bound as I am?"

Among the devils who had possessed the woman there were also the four demons that had formerly been tied in the River Euphrates. They had done great harm to the Church in the past. Even today, as Father Th. remarked, persecutions against the Church are significant.

The Earling case brought many priests and bishops to a more serious consciousness of existing conditions. Many of them had been skeptical and made further inquiries. They came in the spirit of the doubting Thomas, but humbly left with deeper faith.

Father Th., who has had nineteen cases of possession under his care within recent years, seems convinced that present indications point to the beginning of a great battle between Christ and Antichrist. He also seems to have learned that Judas will appear as Antichrist in this manner, that a human person, soon after birth, will be controlled and completely ruled by him. Besides the Antichrist, there will be the false prophet, in reality Lucifer, who will perform wonderful deeds and false miracles. He will not be born of a woman, but will construct a body for himself out of earthly matter in order to plot as a man among men. But the faithful need not fear, for all the powers of heaven with its countless angels will be fighting on their side.

Letter from Dr. John Dundon

Dr. John Dundon, Physician and Surgeon
1228 E. Brady St., Milwaukee, Wis.

Rev. Celestine Kapsner, O. S. B.
St. John's Abbey
Collegeville, Minn.

Dear Father Kapsner:

We wish to indorse your pamphlet "Vade Satana" as a potent aid to faith in the value of sacramentals, relics of the saints, and prayer. No more vivid picture has been presented to us of the losing battle which the great enemy of the human race has been waging against the "camp of Christ". Nothing has made our inconsistent floundering from the "camp of Christ" to the "camp of the devil" appear so absurd. The memory it has instilled of the hatred of Satan and the eternal misery of his permanent army, evokes a continuous inventory of one's life, savoring of the minuteness of the final judgment. That it will save many souls we have no doubt. That some will borrow fruitless fright is also possible, but for them one must say that if the picture is terrible the real thing must be worse. Agony is the lot of all at least once.

Satan has seemed too unreal. It would be a pity if this pamphlet were to be suppressed because some weak souls have been made to sense him more vividly than the author intends.

We were granted an interview with the exorcist, Father Theophilus, after reading your account of the diabolical possession. We treasure the experience as an intimate glimpse into the life of a pious priest very gifted in a specialty which should command the patronage of the medical profession, rather than to be allotted to the realm of superstition or necromancy. We anxiously await his complete report of the Earling case.

Yours very truly,

J. D. Dundon, M. D.

Appendix III: About the Author

Scott Smith is a Catholic author, attorney, and theologian. He and his wife Ashton are the parents of four wild-eyed children and live in their hometown of New Roads, Louisiana.

Check out more of his writing and courses below …

More from Scott Smith

Scott regularly contributes to his blog, The Scott Smith Blog at www.thescottsmithblog.com, WINNER of the 2018-2019 Fisher's Net Award for Best Catholic Blog:

Scott's other books can be found at his publisher's, Holy Water Books, website, holywaterbooks.com, as well as on Amazon

His other books on theology and the Catholic faith include *The Catholic ManBook*, *Everything You Need to Know About Mary But Were Never Taught*, and *Blessed is He Who …* (Biographies of Blesseds). More on these below …

His fiction includes *The Seventh Word*, a pro-life horror novel, and the *Cajun Zombie Chronicles*, the Catholic version of the zombie apocalypse.

Scott has also produced courses on the Blessed Mother and Scripture for All Saints University.

Learn about the Blessed Mary from anywhere and learn to defend your mother! It includes over six hours of video plus a free copy of the next book ... Enroll Now!

Pray the Rosary with St. John Paul II

St. John Paul II said "the Rosary is my favorite prayer." So what could possibly make praying the Rosary even better? Praying the Rosary with St. John Paul II!

This book includes a reflection from John Paul II for every mystery of the Rosary. You will find John Paul II's biblical reflections on the twenty mysteries of the Rosary that provide practical insights to help you not only understand the twenty mysteries but also live them.

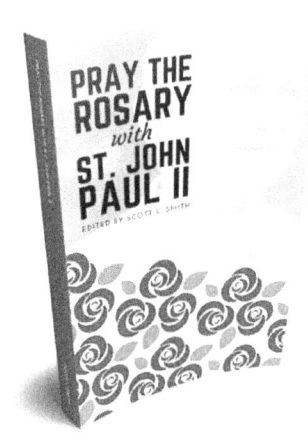

St. John Paul II said "The Rosary is my favorite prayer. A marvelous prayer! Marvelous in its simplicity and its depth. In the prayer we repeat many times the words that the Virgin Mary heard from the Archangel, and from her kinswoman Elizabeth."

St. John Paul II said "the Rosary is the storehouse of countless blessings." In this new book, he will help you dig even deeper into the treasures contained within the Rosary.

You will also learn St. John Paul II's spirituality of the Rosary: "To pray the Rosary is to hand over our burdens to the merciful hearts of Christ and His mother."

"The Rosary, though clearly Marian in character, is at heart a Christ-centered prayer. It has all the depth of the gospel message in its entirety. It is an echo of the prayer of Mary, her perennial Magnificat for the work of the redemptive Incarnation which began in her virginal womb."

Take the Rosary to a whole new level with St. John Paul the Great! St. John Paul II, *pray for us!*

What You Need to Know About Mary But Were Never Taught

Give a robust defense of the Blessed Mother using Scripture. Now, more than ever, every Catholic needs to learn how to defend their mother, the Blessed Mother. Because now, more than ever, the family is under attack and needs its Mother.

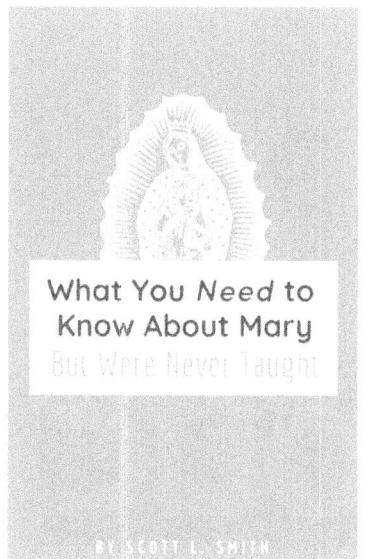

Discover the love story, hidden within the whole of Scripture, of the Father for his daughter, the Holy Spirit for his spouse, and the Son for his MOTHER.

This collection of essays and the All Saints University course made to accompany it will demonstrate through Scripture how the Immaculate Conception of Mary was prophesied in Genesis.

It will also show how the Virgin Mary is the New Eve, the New Ark, and the New Queen of Israel.

Catholic Nerds Podcast

As you might have noticed, Scott is obviously well-credentialed as a nerd. Check out Scott's podcast: the Catholic Nerds Podcast on iTunes, Podbean, Google Play, and wherever good podcasts are found!

The Catholic ManBook

Do you want to reach Catholic Man LEVEL: EXPERT? *The Catholic ManBook* is your handbook to achieving Sainthood, manly Sainthood. Find the following resources inside, plus many others:

- Top Catholic Apps, Websites, and Blogs
- Everything you need to pray the Rosary
- The Most Effective Daily Prayers & Novenas, including the Emergency Novena
- Going to Confession and Eucharistic Adoration like a boss!
- Mastering the Catholic Liturgical Calendar

The Catholic ManBook contains the collective wisdom of The Men of the Immaculata, of saints, priests and laymen, fathers and sons, single and married. Holiness is at your fingertips. Get your copy today.

NEW! This year's edition also includes a revised and updated St. Louis de Montfort Marian consecration. Follow the prayers in a day-by-day format.

The Seventh Word

The FIRST Pro-Life Horror Novel!

Pro-Life hero, Abby Johnson, called it "legit scary ... I don't like reading this as night! ... It was good, it was so good ... it was terrifying, but good."

The First Word came with Cain, who killed the first child of man. The Third Word was Pharaoh's instruction to the midwives. The Fifth Word was carried from Herod to Bethlehem. One of the Lost Words dwelt among the Aztecs and hungered after their children.

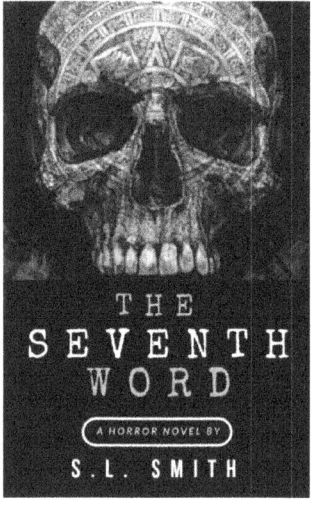

Evil hides behind starched white masks. The ancient Aztec demon now conducts his affairs in the sterile environment of corporate medical facilities. An insatiable hunger draws the demon to a sleepy Louisiana hamlet. There, it contracts the services of a young attorney, Jim David, whose unborn child is the ultimate object of the demon's designs. Monsignor, a mysterious priest of unknown age and origin, labors unseen to save the soul of a small town hidden deep within Louisiana's plantation country, nearly forgotten in a bend of the Mississippi River.

You'll be gripped from start to heart-stopping finish in this page-turning thriller.

With roots in Bram Stoker's Dracula, this horror novel reads like Stephen King's classic stories of towns being slowly devoured by an unseen evil and the people who unite against it.

The book is set in southern Louisiana, an area the author brings to life with compelling detail based on his local knowledge.

Blessed is He Who ...
Models of Catholic Manhood

You are the average of the five people you spend the most time with, so spend more time with the Saints! Here are several men that you need to get to know whatever your age or station in life. These short biographies will give you an insight into how to live better, however you're living.

From Kings to computer nerds, old married couples to single teenagers, these men gave us extraordinary examples of holiness:

- Pier Giorgio Frassati & Carlo Acutis – Here are two extraordinary **young men**, an athlete and a computer nerd, living on either side of the 20th Century
- Two men of royal stock, Francesco II and Archduke Eugen, lived lives of holiness despite all the world conspiring against them.
- There's also the **simple husband and father**, Blessed Luigi. Though he wasn't a king, he can help all of us treat the women in our lives as queens.

Blessed Is He Who ... Models of Catholic Manhood explores the lives of six men who found their greatness in Christ and His Bride, the Church. In six succinct chapters, the authors, noted historian Brian J. Costello and theologian and attorney Scott L. Smith, share with you the uncommon lives of exceptional men who will one day be numbered among the Saints of Heaven, men who can bring all of us closer to sainthood.

THANKS FOR READING! TOTUS TUUS

Made in the USA
Coppell, TX
30 November 2022